NOV 2 9 2004

a city equal to my desire

ALSO BY JAMES SALLIS

THE LONG-LEGGED FLY
MOTH
BLACK HORNET
EYE OF THE CRICKET
BLUEBOTTLE
GHOST OF A FLEA
DEATH WILL HAVE YOUR EYES
RENDERINGS
CYPRESS GROVE
A FEW LAST WORDS (STORIES)
LIMITS OF THE SENSIBLE WORLD (STORIES)
TIME'S HAMMERS: COLLECTED STORIES (STORIES)
LES JOURS EN FEU (STORIES)
SORROW'S KITCHEN (POEMS)
MY TONGUE IN OTHER CHEEKS: SELECTED TRANSLATIONS (POEMS)
ASH OF STARS: ON THE WRITING OF SAMUEL R. DELANY (EDITOR)
JAZZ GUITARS (EDITOR)
THE GUITAR IN JAZZ (EDITOR)
THE GUITAR PLAYERS
DIFFICULT LIVES
SAINT GLINGLIN BY RAYMOND QUENEAU (TRANSLATOR)
GENTLY INTO THE LAND OF THE MEATEATERS
CHESTER HIMES: A LIFE

FORTHCOMING
JAMES SALLIS READER (FROM POINTBLANK)
DRIVE (NOVEL)
OTHERS OF MY KIND (NOVEL)
BLACK NIGHT'S GONNA CATCH ME HERE: SELECTED POEMS 1968-2002 (POEMS)
LEANING INTO THE ELECTRIC DAY (POEMS)

a city equal to my desire

james sallis

introduction by Jack O'Connell

POINT*BLANK*

POINT*BLANK* is an imprint of Wildside Press
PO Box 301, Holicong, PA 18928-0301
www.wildsidepress.com
www.pointblankpress.com

edited by Juha Lindroos

For more information contact Wildside Press

ISBN: 1-930997-67-1 (PB)
ISBN: 1-930997-68-X (HB)

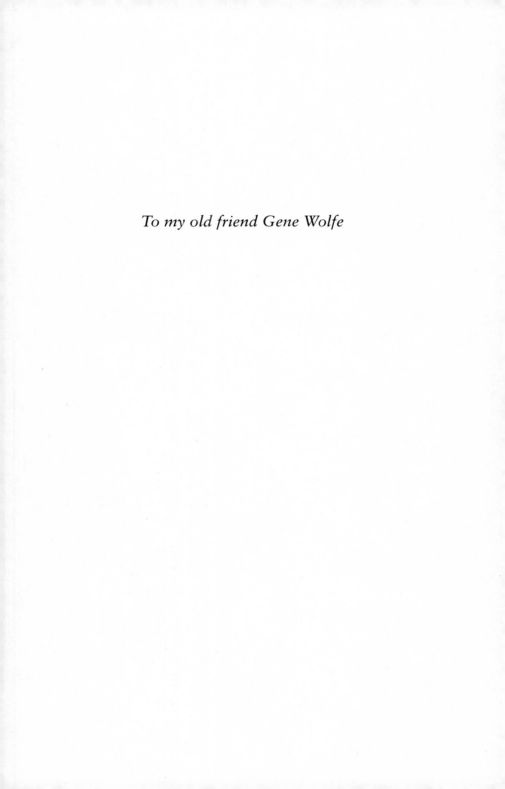

To my old friend Gene Wolfe

contents

the i-ghost and me

an introduction to
A City Equal to My Desire

IN THE DREAM, I am a detective with russet skin and a problematic memory. I am also mildly claustrophobic and my vision occasionally fails me. All of which is worrisome in that I am trapped inside a crowd, Fat Tuesday's throng, trying to solve a puzzle, find a clue. I am imprisoned within a mob, searching for something lost. The precise nature of the lost object remains at the edge of my consciousness, always just beyond revelation. Later, driving to the diner, I mulled the possibilities: A missing lover. A missing father. A missing child. In the parking lot, I thought for a moment that the object of my search might have been something as old fashioned and obvious as my own true identity.

The problem, as always, is that the dream was ruptured by the phone call before I could resolve anything. N passed me the receiver. Downstairs, the dog let out a howl, but, thankfully, the children remained asleep.

Sallis spoke in a voice that was friendly and wide-awake.

"I'm told," he said, "that the intro is done."

I came out of the fog instantly and glanced at the clock on the nightstand.

"What time is it where you are?" I asked.

He ignored the question—he'd been asked it too many times by fans and dim-witted journalists.

"Our friend in New Albany says the introduction is finished," he said. "I thought that maybe we could meet."

In that instant, I knew he was in the city. I swung my legs out of bed, started reaching around the dark of the floor for my jeans.

"Name the place," I said, my nervousness making me think for a second that I might rise to any of his challenges.

On the other end, it sounded as if he were coughing or laughing with a hand clapped over the mouth of the phone. When his voice came on again, he said, "It's your town, buddy."

Once again, I'd forgotten. My wife rolled onto her stomach, pulled the pillow over her head.

I gave him directions to the Central Diner from the highway, not entirely sure, as I counted off the intersections and rail crossings, it would be open.

"I'll find my way," he said and hung up.

I racked the phone, pulled a jacket off the doorknob and grabbed my keys from the bureau. Downstairs, in the kitchen, I hushed the dog and made my way to the refrigerator. I pulled open the freezer door and moved boxes of popsicles and frozen waffles, till I could reach the manuscript of the book that you hold in your hands.

Rolling out of the driveway, I instinctively turned on the radio. Catching myself, I dialed it off, eased the car out to the street and brought myself back to the stories and their maker. Once again, we find ourselves stranded in a time of war and plague, stupidity and amnesia. Once again, the only solution is to embrace the stories like a lover who can forgive any slight as she heals every wound.

I forget this too often. Sallis has never forgotten it. He has lived his life as if this truth had been tattooed on his knuckles at birth. And in this way, I confess, he shames me just a little.

Uncomfortable with the thought, I concentrated on the drive, decided to stick to the back roads, ignore the highway, its lights and its noise. Perhaps I should have directed him to my house. But the dog is a high-strung terrier and would have been all over him. What was it that Basho said about the danger of the beast humping the shadow?

Besides, it *had* to be the Central, because, though he can't know it, this was where our bond was first sutured.

IT WAS A good 10 years ago. A Wednesday in November. Thanksgiving Eve, in fact. Cold and raw in the way only rust belt New England can manage. The sky was slate gray and threatening our unique brand of sleet, a mixture of ice and the creosote that had become a permanent part of my city's skies long before my birth.

The weather was playing metaphor to my mood: I'd spent the previous weeks, maybe months, wrestling with the same juvenile questions about identity and purpose until they'd become a swarm of parasites just under my skin—crawling, biting, raging with the primal hunger of gangrene. By midday, I knew I had to clear out of this burg for a while. The radio gave up some West African blues, which seemed oddly appropriate as I roamed the forgotten towns that rimmed my home, trying to find a place to land.

That I wound up at the Central Diner was nothing but luck. That the joint was empty was a small chunk of grace that I didn't deserve. I parked and reached around into the back seat, where I kept a milk crate that I filled with paperbacks in the same manner that my peers housed their hammers and wrenches. I put my hand in blind and pulled out a thin volume—*Difficult Lives*.

Today, I can't recall where it came from. Maybe Mark Ziesing's catalog? Maybe Otto Penzler's Mysterious Bookshop? I'd like to think that it had been mailed to me, anonymously, by some noir angel, patron and protector of gutter scribes everywhere. Right there at the start, I grabbed it reflexively, like a motel bible, and entered the diner.

I don't recall what I ate that day. I know that I drank more coffee than even the shoddiest medical association would have sanctioned. I believe the lone waitress/cook realized the intensity of the experience I was having with the book and, beyond refilling my mug, kept her distance and made herself busy cleaning the steam wells.

Gorgeously written, Sallis's essays on the tortured lives and books of Thompson, Goodis and Himes was, for me, a baptism. In the hours that I made my way through its pages, as the ashy snow covered the lunch car and the wind shook its railroad windows, I was given my name and my work. I understand that this will read as melodramatic. But that's often the risk of telling the truth about a conversion. And so be it.

I drove home that night through the accumulating blizzard in a calm, interior fog. The scabies under the skin were gone, exorcized by a gospel about subversive genre scribblers. I entered the house feeling clean and, let me say it, healed, the book under my coat, near my heart. I climbed up to my attic office, sat behind the desk and stared at the author's name: *Sallis*.

It strummed a chord somewhere back in the brain. But, again, a lifetime of fiction had done things less than benign to my memory. So I did what I tend to do when confused. I let instinct guide me. I moved to the wall of books opposite my desk and began pulling down volumes.

Within 30 minutes I found what I had not known I'd been looking for in *Again, Dangerous Visions*, one of the landmark anthologies of the early '70s, which codified the notion of an American "New Wave" in science fiction.

A,DV had been one of my signal texts. We'd found each other at exactly the right time. I was in the early days of an angry adolescence. Beyond the standard hormonal madness, much of that anger was the result of a chronic and virulent frustration and panic born of the growing certainty that, though I wanted nothing more out of life than to become a writer, I had no notion of how one accomplished this feat. I didn't know any writers. My world was circumscribed by my insulated, isolated factory city. It was populated by mill workers, cops, electricians, priests, salesmen and lunatics. By the age of 12, I'd just about convinced myself that some obscure law of physics determined that one could not originate in my hometown and grow into a writer. That there was a natural filter or some stunting agent, in the water or the air, that precluded a writing life.

In order to fight against that panic, I collected bits and pieces of lore and rumor from the fringes of the writing life. It was like living in the desert and listening hard, always, for the faintest traces of bells ringing in Zion. I would memorize as if gospel the thumbnail author's biographies printed on the rear covers of the paperbacks that I purchased at the corner Rexall. I would read and reread the "Jack London" entry in the public library's *Britannica*. I would study the movements of Rob Petrie—TV's only writer-hero—as he pecked away on the office manual typewriter, trapped forever in rerun. These long-shot glimpses created a desperate and ludicrous rosary, which I used to petition my i-ghost.

The word is my own creation, a contraction of "iconic ghost." And I coined it many years after I built its referent. From this distance, I can see, of course, that I constructed the i-ghost, methodically and secretly, but also, mostly unconsciously, in the manner that we build our most precious daydreams. The i-ghost was my assemblage of all the features, attitudes, personality traits that I imagined were possessed by the wandering, American writer. I constructed the ghost from the rough parts I had on hand, then worked him without mercy, forced him to be part muse, part patron saint, and part outrider—an advance scout leading the way through foreign territory, cutting my path, pointing toward a literary Canaan on the horizon.

At age 12, with the discovery of *Again, Dangerous Visions*, my i-ghost was transformed from the muddy lump of unconscious personal archetype into the golum of my hyper-conscious hopes and dreams. Harlan Ellison's vivid introductions to each story in the anthology made the story's writer come alive for me. Late in the night, as my younger brother slept deeply in the bed next to mine, I found a teeming, transient colony of mad scribes, visionaries every one: Hip. Cool. Independent. Roving the land. Living by their wits and their talent and their dreams.

Those *AD,V* intros were the current that animated my i-ghost. And when he climbed off the table of my unconscious and stepped out of the shadows and into the glare of my headboard reading lamp, I discovered that he was dressed in the clothes of James Sallis.

Sallis was the only writer in the anthology who rated two stories and in the intro, Ellison compared him to Fitzgerald, Dylan Thomas and Randall Jarrell. That brief portrait sketched a rambling artist, a dangerous, maybe violent, trickster launching surreal myths at the ground zero of an imploding zeitgeist. He appeared part spy to me—furtive, mobile and mysterious. Landing in New York and crashing at the Algonquin Hotel on a shaky credit card, carrying a book of French poetry and (I loved this part) a Mickey Spillane novel. In the morning, he's off to Poland. In between now and then, he beds a phantom woman and writes a refusal to comment on his latest work.

Eureka!

I had found my role model.

I had discovered my outrider.

I had given flesh to my i-ghost.

Had the moment occurred in a story, some earnest *bildungsroman*, the reader would never make it to the end of the tale, finding such a device too pat, too easy, too romantic and artificial. Thankfully, the i-ghost presented himself not on the pages of some coming-of-age fable, but in the midst of my anxious twelfth year.

From that moment on, there was no looking back. I knew I'd follow my i-ghost into the territories. And more than this, I knew that as long as I kept an eye on his shadow, I would never get lost. I may have forgotten his name over the ensuing years, chasing him across broken trails. But I never forgot my sense, my visceral perception, of his essence.

And so, 20 years later, as I rediscovered the name and identity of the i-ghost, I felt the chill of a long-delayed recognition. This Sallis had shaped my notion of the person that I wanted to become and the life I wanted to embody.

I felt, on the floor of my attic study, under its slanting eaves, on that cold November night, the chill associated with the most primal of our emotions and imaginations. It is, I suppose, too much altogether to compare my chill with the shiver of the lost child encountering the unknown father. But I'd argue that my feeling that night was located somewhere in the bleachers of that particular ballpark.

That chill marked the beginning of a series of coincidences—maybe even synchronicities—that would occur periodically over the next decade. And culminate back at the Central Diner at 3 A.M. on a nameless morning last week that has already begun to feel less than real, but much more than a false memory.

When my novel, *Word Made Flesh*, was published several years ago, the silence that greeted its arrival was shattered by a review that was everything I could have hoped for and more besides—one of those lifelines that hoists you from the muck of self-doubt and lost faith and drops you back at your desk. The kind of generous slap that wakes you, explains you to yourself all over again, and sets you back on your only course. I felt the chill when I realized that the review was penned by Jim Sallis.

Weeks later, after reading the review, I found myself in France, walking with my publisher along the promenade that bordered the beach along the Brittany coast. We were approached by a group of carousing bookmen – editors, reviewers, translators. Introductions were made. The last individual with whom I shook hands was, you know it, Jim Sallis. I have no idea what I said to him that night. I recall only the now-familiar chill as he disappeared into the fog of Saint-Malo surrounded by a ring of Gallic admirers.

BUT HE IS not, of course, only smoke and rumor. There is, as they say, a *vita* behind the legend. And over the last 10 years, I've collected some facts and figures, though I can't guarantee at this time which ones are true:

He was born in 1944 on 21 December, the birth date of Thomas Becket, Racin and Frank Zappa. The date on which the Pilgrims landed at Plymouth Rock and the Curies discovered radium and Elvis traveled to his infamous summit with Nixon. Jim's father, Mr. Chappelle Horace Sallis, labored as a clerk. His mother, a city clerk, the former Miss Mildred Liming, looked after her boys. An older sibling, John, paved the way for his kid brother by being a genius who knew that the world was bigger, deeper and much more mysterious than even the darkest corner of Helena, Arkansas, could hint.

One rumor has it that Jim Sallis left home at 17, shook the sand of the Natural State from his feet and never looked back. Others speculate that he has been carrying his own fat wallet of Southern history with him since he hit that first road. While there's no yearbook photo to confirm it, he seems to have spent some time at Tulane—though I can't manage to imagine him cheering on the Green Wave or pledging to Delta Tau Delta.

He married young and fathered a son. He divorced young and traveled widely. He worked all the requisite dust jacket gigs—did some teaching, lots of editing and reviewing. He remarried and immersed himself, deeply, in studies of music and language. He read every goddamn thing he could get his hands on. He found his people and threw in with them: Dostoevsky and Camus, Robbe-Grillet and Queneau, Boris Vian and Chester Himes, Theodore Sturgeon and Alberta Hunter.

Though not necessarily in this order, residual evidence indicates he has lived in London; Boston; New York; Milford, Penn.; Arlington, Texas; Somewhere, Iowa. He has written of time spent in a psychiatric ward. He has written of days spent wandering an American city, broke and hungry. He recommends the experience as a requirement for holding public office. It instilled in him—or, more likely, enlarged—a reservoir of empathy that will always inform his work in a crucial way. But wherever he found himself, through whatever vagaries life rained down upon him, he wrote. Stories, novels, poems, essays and, I'm pretty certain, some terrifying mountain of letters. Twenty-three books thus far. As he wrote to me a year or so ago (when I had whined about a seemingly terminal bout of stagnation):

> What I do is, I sit down here, with my ever-spreading, ever-more-static butt in the chair, and I write. Most days I think what I write sucks huge, huge rocks. Other days I think That ain't bad. Then when I read it all a year or so later I can't tell one day from another. Here's the secret: Those of us who aim so high set ourselves for failure; it's self-fulfilling prophecy. We just have to find that one thing or that handful of things we do that no one else can do, and keep on doing them.

They say he's hunkered down on the edge of the desert these days, in the land of lizards and cacti. But to my mind, his physical locale is almost always irrelevant. Because his mind, the fount of all his work, exists forever, I'm sure, in that space where the essential, universal story breeds with the singular imagination to produce an oeuvre that I'm tempted to label *sacramental*. I know that others will disagree, quickly and maybe violently, with my word choice here. There's a good chance that Sallis will, as well. But I'm trusting that, as one of his readers, he owes—and will slice me—a little slack. And, beyond this, I sense that he will understand (if not endorse) my proposition that he is simultaneously empiricist *and* gnostic. Which might be only another way of restating that he is, in the best and truest sense, a shaman, an outrider, an i-ghost. That is, the kind of writer whose collective work is never content to comprehend, reflect and chronicle our consensus reality, but is compelled to turn that reality inside out to reveal—perhaps even revel in—its flaws, its gaps in logic and integrity.

As you'll see in a few moments, Sallis is part poker player and part magician. His face gives away nothing but his hands are always in motion. Like the old pop song advises, his methodology often requires him to be cruel in order to be kind. This is how you know that he's the artist in the room full of dilettantes and poseurs. He'll pay any cost, take any chance, to work his hoodoo on you.

Understand this: Sallis wants to take your experience of the world, mutate it to the edge of recognition, and then deliver it back before your eyes like a coin pulled from behind your earlobe. And in this way, he makes you see and feel, all over again, the meaning, the beauty—and, pointedly sometimes, the horror—of being human.

And yet, even as I've come to understand large chunks of his history and smaller nuggets of his mission, he remains part myth to me. And maybe some percentage of my wish, as I rolled to a stop in front of the Central Diner last week, was to reduce him to flesh. Because I've come to believe that, at some point, it is necessary to say goodbye to one's i-ghost, to set him free from the strictures and obligations of your interior mythology. To become an adult and make your own way.

THE CENTRAL WAS much as I'd remembered it. An older diner, it was an original creation of the Worcester Lunchcar Company, and, so, small and warm, inherently cozy. It had a barrel ceiling made of gleaming wood and featuring an antique tin paddle fan that was turning too slowly to move the air. The counter was a gray marble slab shot through with black veins. There was a minimum of stainless steel—the walls were all baked porcelain with a mahogany trim to which there were tacked menu cards (franks & beans, $2.50) and Marine Corps recruiting posters. The floor was ancient but clean, Spanish tile in a checkerboard pattern. There were five tiny, two-man booths flush against the exterior wall. I went to the last one and slid into it under the bored gaze of the proprietress, a stooped crone whose lack of a hair net may or may not be a health code violation but, in either case, was unsettling. I could not decide if she was the same woman who had served me on my first visit to the diner. She wore a uniform of some sort, a white smock more suited to nursing than the culinary arts and dating from another era. Pinned above her left breast was a white plastic nameplate that told me this was "Audrey."

From the booth, I met her stare and said, "I'm waiting for someone," as if she had asked.

She nodded her acceptance of the situation and turned to fiddle with the mammoth Bunn-O-Matic coffee urn.

There in the booth, the weight of the night's significance began to overwhelm me. Flustered, trying to distract myself, I grabbed a newspaper off the table and opened it. It was an alternative freebie, a weekly arts sheet with a lengthy section of personal ads. Sometimes I read the ads as if they are radically abbreviated short stories. But that night, edgy with anticipation, I just didn't have the stomach for so much raw loneliness.

Instead, I opened to the movie page. The Oxford Drive-In was showing a double-feature: *Out of the Past* and *Last Year at Marienbad*. I kept my eyes off the crone, tore the ad out deliberately and slid it into my jacket pocket. And then, unable to stop myself, I opened Sallis's still cold manuscript one more time and began to leaf through it, stopping now and then to run my fingers down a paragraph, reread a bit of dialogue or a line of description.

Again, I was struck by the genuine boldness, the confidence of the longtime pro, unafraid to jump in and out of diverse genres and styles, to take what he needs and leave what he doesn't. To trick out what he's taken, turn a widget into a diamond with a pass of the hand and a whispered conjuration. There is a furious counter-cultural impulse in Sallis's work. It's just under the skin of these stories. It demands that some things should reside beyond the reach of the market. And it insists that if we cannot embrace ambiguity, we must, at very least, acknowledge it.

The pages sliding under my eyes were testament to a unique and, finally, unexplainable mixture of instinct, vision and voice. These were the words, I sensed, of what they used to call an adult. These were the stories of an outrider who has gone farther than you and I. Who knows more than you and I about desire and loss, identity and rage, solitude and love.

Consider this sentence: Then she came into my life like a nail into cork.

Don't you love that line? It is the work of a man who knows how to help people breathe. Who has known the kind of grief that can turn a human into stone and who has resisted the transformation. And it was the line I was rereading when Audrey appeared, carrying two bone white plates of what looked like Western omelets and—*Could it be? This far north?*—grits.

I looked up at her as I closed the manuscript and said, "I didn't order this."

She nodded and put one plate down in front of me, another opposite me, and said, "No, you didn't. But he did."

And her head motioned toward my window, which was almost obscured by a covering of white moths. Through an open nickel of glass, I could see the car idling next to my own out in the lot. I hadn't heard him pull in. And how the hell could he have ordered these omelets?

He was driving what looked like a 20-year-old Dodge, brown, but with a big splash of silver primer paint on the driver's door. Bought, I sensed, just for this trip. To be sold, I sensed, halfway through the next journey. I turned and got up on my knees in the booth, glanced through the grime of his windshield and thought I saw a scuffed up leather duffel and a copy of *Calligrammes* resting on the passenger seat. I wondered if there were a steel guitar, maybe a clawhammer banjo, in the trunk.

I turned back in my seat just in time to see him come through the door of the diner like the hero of a classic spaghetti western. He was wearing the clothes of his profession—a faded leather jacket, a denim shirt, jeans. And were those desert boots?

I've seen a photo of him, a black & white snapshot, taken at the Milford Writer's Conference in 1967. A candid portrait, it came to my mind as he appeared before me: Sallis is 23 years old, posed between Michael Moorcock, who looks like a fun-loving bloke out of some Nottingham kitchen sink drama, and Damon Knight, who looks like a folk singing engineer on holiday. And then there's young James, dressed in a sport coat with elbow patches of leather or suede and a mustache that looks like it could go Fu Manchu on him inside a month. He wears eyeglasses and, tellingly, his hands are tucked behind his back. To me, it appears as if he's ready to split this scene, toss his portable Olympia into the convertible Mustang and burn some rubber on his way out of town. He looks, in other words, like the embodiment of the i-ghost.

Thirty-seven years later, stepping into the Central Diner, it was obvious that all the barely contained erudition and energy remained. He wore a beard and wire-rim glasses. There was a pen clipped inside the pocket of his shirt and I tried and failed to see the brand. And there was a bottle of Lagavulin under his arm.

Without being asked, Audrey brought two water glasses and placed them on the table. Sallis filled the glasses, two fingers each, raised his toward me and quoted an old blues.

"To the city of refuge."

"Blind Willie Reynolds," I said, trying to attribute the line.

"Blind Willie *Johnson*," he said, correcting me.

We both took a drink and then he sat down opposite me, picked up a fork without hesitation and dug into his eggs.

"What is it about an omelet," he asked, "that makes it the perfect road food?"

I let the question stand as rhetorical.

Fork halfway to his mouth, he suddenly looked at the window behind me. I thought he was about to comment on the infestation of moths. Turned out he was staring past the moths at the abandoned and half-destroyed factory across the street, lit up viciously by the moon. He said, "Christ, this place makes Utica look like Paris."

I smiled but I couldn't bring up the laugh. It was too late and already the Scotch was triggering my Celtic impulse toward the morose.

"Our minds repeat the landscape," I quoted him to himself—a nasty trick I thought I'd outgrown.

I expected a smile, but he only shrugged.

"It's like Jimmy Feibleman always said," he replied. "*When you find yourself in post-historic times, all you can do is dream.*"

And, bang, I felt the old chill again because the fact is I had Feibleman's *Technology & Reality* out in the backseat milk crate. As always, the coincidence pushed me to get to the point.

"What's the deal, Jim?" I ask. "Why'd you come all this way?"

"I told you. I came to pick up the introduction, " he said. "You know the problem with writers? They always look for the ulterior motive. It's a professional hazard."

"From where I sit, " I said, "it's just good policy."

"Tomāto," he said, "Tomăto. You know, when I started the last Lew Griffin book, I didn't know it would be the finale. Lew had to clue me in."

"Meaning?" I asked.

"Meaning," he said, and paused to sip his Scotch, "that the art of the exit is difficult and beautiful and mysterious. And worth learning well."

"I'm not sure I understand," I said.

"Well, if confusion were a crime, we'd all be serving life."

"Skip James?" I tried.

"I think that one," he said, "belongs to Frances Farmer." And then, suddenly switching from Zen master to Dutch Uncle, he asked "What's the situation with the Vicodin?"

I hesitated, wondering how he knew. Then I managed to say, "I'm weaning."

"Are you working?" he asked.

"Trying," I said, "to finish a new one."

"About?" he asked, baiting me sweetly, knowing, to his core, what a dilemma that question is for the writer.

I shrugged, as he knew I would. But then I surprised him by answering.

"It's about entombment," I said.

He nodded his approval.

"And bikers," I added, as if afraid my first answer hadn't been enough.

"Bikers," he said, "are always good."

He finished his Scotch, took a breath, reveling in the aroma of fried eggs and onions and burnt coffee, a smell that, I trust, will forever define my city for him.

"Keep working," he told me.

He got up and brought his empty glass to the counter so that Audrey wouldn't have to bus it. I watched him whisper softly to her as he slid some money onto the counter. And I realized that, if he is a mysterious stranger, a nomadic drifter out of a noir fable, he is also, in person, a kind of displaced Southern gentleman, perpetually polite and gracious. Though he long ago banished the accent, a sense of easy civility remains steadfast.

He returned to the booth but didn't sit down.

"What we do," he said, "is important. It matters."

I looked down at the balance of my omelet and said, "I'd be embarrassed to tell you how often I forget that."

He pulled his jacket out of the booth and slid into it.

"*That*," he said, "is what I drove all this fucking way to tell you."

I had no response. And he let my silence underline the seriousness of his message.

He lifted the manuscript off the Formica, tucked it under his arm and touched my shoulder.

But I wanted to prolong the moment. So, like some 16-year-old, drunk on hope and fear, I reached into my pocket and pulled out the ad for the double-feature at the Oxford Drive-In. I slid it across the table, it's ragged edge turning dark as it picked up a spilled droplet of Scotch.

He studied the ad, but shook his head, demurred. I nodded my understanding, but I thought, *Maybe if it had been a different movie? Maybe if one of the features had been* Point Blank? *Could even Sallis refuse Lee Marvin?*

Then, without explanation, he folded the newsprint and slid it into his shirt pocket and my spirits were lifted with the possibility that, perhaps, just maybe, he'd use it in some capacity. I'd find the reference one day, like a blues lyric or a line from Sauser or Vian, in one of his stories.

And he walked out of the diner.

Through the window, the moths suddenly vanished, I watched him move to his car. Did I imagine a limp, an old injury, dating back to childhood? Maybe the vestige of a long-ago summer day spent reading Leiber and Bester in a fig tree while Sonny Boy Williamson played on a radio in the distance? Maybe the fracture that transpired when some heartbreakingly wonderful passage caused the boy to forget where he was and plummet to the earth, another victim of gravity.

But no. It was just a stutter-step. Probably just a story idea being delivered. A line from a poem breaking into the world and causing a chill in its vessel. Or maybe it was only my own overheated imagination, wanting to conceive the labors of his creation in terms of a physical cost.

I watched him unlock the Dodge and open the door. In the waning moonlight, the silver patch of primer seemed to glow. Sallis began to climb behind the wheel. Then turned and glanced at me, framed in the diner's front window.

He brought a hand up to his forehead, his fingers tight together but cupped as if to scratch an itch. He touched their tips against his brow and then brought the hand out into the night air. A kind of poet's salute. And then he mouthed something. A short word. A single syllable, I'd guess. I want to believe it was a name.

I stared, unblinking, as he backed the Dodge out of the lot and drove away, into the shadows. He is headed, I'm certain, for the city of stories, a place so teeming, so vast, that it promises to contain our communal desire for meaning. What he's doing, this outrider, the gyrovague, is charting our course. And all we have to do is turn the page, cross the border and follow him into the city.

You hold his latest fictions in your hands. They will take you wherever it is that you need to go.

Trust me on this.

Go now.

Follow his shadow and embrace the chill he ignites. You are in the hands of a master whose method for ransoming himself will redeem you in the bargain. And isn't that more than you could desire? Isn't that a grace bigger than any city you have ever known?

Jack O'Connell
May 2004

Ukulele and the World's Pain

SURE, I KILLED the son of a bitch. I mean, what right did he think he had, bursting out in laughter like that when I took Miss Shelley out of her case? I'm a professional, too. I was getting scale just like him. I've paid my union dues and a lot more dues besides.

It was a good date. Sonny Martin had made a name for himself in country music, and now he was doing what he'd been talking about doing for years, he was cutting a jazz album. I'd played on a couple of Martin sessions before. He liked the freshness of the sound, I guess. And he knew that jazz was my first love, too. One time during a session break, I remember, I think this was on his album *Longneck Love*, we started goofing on "Don't Get Around Much Anymore," just the two of us, and before we knew, everybody else had picked his instrument back up and was playing along.

Playing music's not about making sounds, you know, it's about listening. Everything unfolds out of the first note, that first attack.

Sonny always reminded me a lot of the great George Barnes, just this plain, balding, fat guy with a Barcalounger and two or three cheap suits at home doing his job, only his job happened to be, instead of working as an auto mechanic or Sears salesman, recording country hits. Or in this case, playing great jazz and backup. You half-expected a cigar stump to be sticking out of his mouth there above the Gibson.

By contrast, the guy who thought Miss Shelley was so funny was a real Bubba type with stringy hair, glasses that kept sliding down his nose and getting pushed back up, and run-over white shoes with plastic buckles most of the gold paint had come off of. He played a fair guitar, but you know what? That's not enough. Besides him, there was a drummer who looked vaguely familiar and couldn't have been more than nineteen, the great, loose Morty Epstein on bass, and a pianist who gave the impression of spending more time in concert halls than with the likes of us.

We slammed around on a 12-bar shuffle just to start the thing running and get acquainted, and that went well, with the guitar sliding in these little pulls, bends and stumbling, broken runs way up high—Sonny's guitar was so solid Bubba could float. But towards the end he left off that and, staying high, started strumming on just two or three strings, looking over at me.

Sonny called "Sweet Georgia Brown" and we worked it through a time or two by ear, kind of clanging and clunking along, then Sonny had the guitar player scribble out some quick charts. I got mine and we started running it and a line or two in, looking ahead, I can see it's wrong. So I just played right on past it, grinning at the guitar player the whole time. As we started winding down, Sonny nodded me in for a solo. I took a chorus and it was pretty hot and he signalled for another and that one was steaming, and then we all took off again. I looked over and the piano man's staring at me, shaking his head, fingers going on about their business there below. Looks like he just ate a cat.

Next we worked up a head version of a slow, ballady blues, then put some time in on jamming "Take the A Train" and "Lulu's Back in Town." Again Bubba threw some charts together and again mine was wrong—wildly wrong this time. He did everything but hop keys on me. I don't know, maybe his mother was frightened by some Hawaiian when he was in there in the womb growing that greasy hair and trying on those white shoes.

That's where Miss Shelley and her kin came from—you all know that. But you probably don't know much more. That it emerged around 1877, most likely as a derivative of a four-string folk guitar, the *machada* or *machete*, introduced to the islands by the Portuguese. Or how it hitched a ride back to the U.S. with returning sailors and soldiers. Martin started selling them in 1916; Gibson, Regal, Vega, Harmony and Kay all offered standard to premium models alongside their guitars, banjos and mandolins; National manufactured resonator ukes. Briefly, banjo ukuleles came into favor. Other variations include the somewhat larger taropatch, an eight-string uke of paired strings, and the tiple, whose two outer courses of steel strings are doubled, with an additional third string added to the two inner courses and tuned an octave lower. Mario Maccaferri, the man who designed the great Django Reinhardt's guitar, after losing half a million or so with plastic guitars no one would buy, recouped with sale of some nine million plastic ukes. And the players! The ever-amazing Roy Smeck. Cliff Edwards, known as Ukulele Ike. Or Lyle Ritz. Trained on violin, he was a top studio bass player in the 60s and 70s and turned out three astonishing albums of straightahead jazz ukulele.

We worked through what we had again, then broke for lunch. Morty and I grabbed hot dogs at the taco stand by the park across the street and sat on a bench catching up. The fountain was clogged with food wrappers, leaves and cigarette butts as usual. Kids in swings were shoved screaming towards the sky. Old men sat on benches tossing stale bread at pigeons. Morty's son had just started college all the way up in Iowa, he told me, studying physical chemistry, whatever that was. Better be looking for more gigs, I said. He shook his head. Don't I know it, he said. Don't I know it. I told Morty I had a quick errand that couldn't wait, I'd see him inside.

Well, we got back from lunch break, as you know, everybody but the guitar player, and after we wait a while and drink up a pot of coffee Sonny says: Anybody see Walt out there? But none of us know him, of course, and who'd want to look at that greasy hair while he was eating?

So we—Sonny, I should say—finally called the session off, shut it down. And I do regret that. Some fine music was *this close* to being cut.

Can I tell you one thing before we go?

There's this story about Eric Dolphy. He's called in to overdub on a session. Brings all his instruments along. He listens to the tape and what he does is he adds this single note, on bass clarinet, right at the end. That's it. He collects scale for the session, puts his horn back in the case, and goes home. But what he did there, what that one note was, was Dolphy finding his holy moment, you know? That's what we're all looking for, what we go on looking for, that single holy moment, all our lives.

Drive

As I sd to my
friend, because I am
always talking,—John, I

sd, which was not his
name, the darkness sur-
rounds us, what

can we do against
it, or else, shall we &
why not, buy a goddamn big car,

drive, he sd, for
christ's sake, look
out where yr going.

Robert Creeley

MUCH LATER, AS he sat with his back against an inside wall of a Motel 6 just north of Phoenix, watching the pool of blood lap toward him, Driver would wonder whether he had made a terrible mistake. Later still, of course, there'd be no doubt. But for now Driver is, as they say, in the moment. And the moment includes this blood lapping toward him, the pressure of dawn's late light at windows and door, traffic sounds from the interstate nearby, the sound of someone weeping in the next room.

The blood was coming from the woman, the one who called herself Blanche and claimed to be from New Orleans even when everything about her except the put-on accent screamed East Coast—Bensonhurst, maybe, or some other far reach of Brooklyn. Blanche's shoulders lay across the bathroom door's threshhold. Not much of her head left in there: he knew that.

Their room was 212, second floor, foundation and floors close enough to plumb that the pool of blood advanced slowly, tracing the contour of her body just as he had, moving toward him like an accusing finger. His arm hurt like a son of a bitch. This was the other thing he knew: it would be hurting a hell of a lot more soon.

Driver realized then that he was holding his breath. Listening for sirens, for the sound of people gathering on stairways or down in the parking lot, for the scramble of feet beyond the door as others arrived and stood there, waiting, poised. If there were others.

Once again Driver's eyes swept the room. Near the half-open front door a body lay, that of a skinny, tallish man, possibly an albino. Oddly, not much blood there. Maybe it was only waiting. Maybe when they lifted him, turned him, it would all come pouring out at once. But for now, only the dull flash of neon and headlights off pale skin.

The second body was in the bathroom, lodged securely in the window from outside. That's where Driver had found him, unable to move forward or back. This one had carried a shotgun. Blood from his neck had gathered in the sink below, a thick pudding. Driver used a straight razor when he shaved. It had been his father's. Whenever he moved into a new room, he set out his things first. The razor had been there by the sink, lined up with toothbrush and comb.

Just the two so far. From the first, the guy jammed in the window, he'd taken the shotgun that felled the second. It was a Remington 870, barrel cut down to the length of the magazine, fifteen inches maybe. He knew that from a *Mad Max* rip-off he'd worked on. Driver paid attention.

Now he waited. Listening. For the sound of feet, sirens, slammed doors.

What he heard was the drip of the tub's faucet in the bathroom. Then something else as well. Something scratching, scrabbling. . . .

Some time passed before he realized it was his own arm jumping involuntarily, knuckles rapping on the floor, fingers scratching and thumping as the hand contracted.

Then the sounds stopped. No feeling at all left in the arm, no movement. It hung there, apart from him, unconnected, like an abandoned shoe. Driver willed it to move. Nothing happened.

Worry about that later.

He looked back at the open door. Maybe that's it, Driver thought. Maybe no one else is coming, maybe it's over. Maybe, for now, three bodies are enough.

UP TO THE time Driver got his growth about age twelve, he was small for his age, an attribute of which his father made full use. The boy could fit easily through small openings, bathroom windows, pet doors and so on, making him a considerable helpmate at his father's trade, which happened to be burglary. When he did get his growth he got it all at once, shooting up from just below four feet to six-two almost overnight, it seemed. He'd been something of a stranger to and in his body ever since. When he walks, his arms flail about and he shambles. If he tries to run, often as not he'll trip and fall over. One thing he can do, though, is drive. And he drives like a son of a bitch.

Once he'd got his growth, his father had little use for him. His father had had little use for his mother for a lot longer. So Driver wasn't surprised when one night at the dinner table she went after his old man with butcher and bread knives, one in each fist like a ninja in a red-checked apron. She had one ear off and a wide red mouth drawn in his throat before he could set his coffee cup down. Driver watched, then went on eating his sandwich: Spam and mint jelly on toast. That was about the extent of his mother's cooking.

He'd always marvelled at the force of this docile, silent woman's attack—as though her entire life had gathered toward that single, sudden bolt of action. She was never good for much else afterwards. Driver did what he could. But eventually the state came in and prised her from the crusted filth of an overstuffed chair complete with antimacassar. Driver they packed off to foster parents who right up till the day he left registered surprise whenever he came through the front door or emerged from the tiny attic room where he lived like a wren.

A few days before his sixteenth birthday, Driver came down the stairs from that attic room with all his possessions in a duffel bag and the spare key to the Ford Galaxie. His foster father was at work, his foster mother off conducting classes at Vacation Bible School where, two or three years back, before he stopped going, Driver won the prize for memorizing the most scripture. It was mid-summer, unbearably hot up in his room, not much better down here in the kitchen, and drops of sweat fell onto the note as he wrote it.

> I'm sorry about the car, but I have to have wheels.
> I haven't taken anything else. Thank you for taking
> me in, for everything you've done. I mean that.

Throwing the duffel bag over the seat, he backed out of the garage, pulled up by the stop sign at the end of the street, and made a hard left to California.

THEY MET AT a low-rent bar between Sunset and Hollywood, east of Highland. Uniformed Catholic schoolgirls waited for buses across from a lace, leather and lingerie store and shoe shops full of spike heels size 15 up. He knew the guy right away when he stepped through the door. Pressed chinos, T-shirt, sport coat with sleeves pushed up. *De rigueur* gold wristwatch. Copse of rings at finger and ear. Soft jazz spread from the jukebox, a piano trio, possibly a quartet, something rhythmically slippery, you couldn't quite get a hold on it.

He grabbed a neat whiskey, Driver stayed with what he had, and they went to a table near the back. Driver dropped the shot glass of vodka, like a depth bomb, into his beer.

"What I hear is, you're the best."

"I am."

"Other thing I hear is you can be hard to work with."

"Not if we understand one another."

"What's to understand? I run the team, I call all the shots. Either you sign on to the team or you don't."

"Okay. Then I don't."

Guy threw back what remained of his whiskey and went to the bar for a new round.

"Care to tell me why?" he asked, setting down a new beer and shot.

"I drive. That's *all* I do. I don't sit in while you're planning it or running it down. I don't take part, I don't know anyone, I don't carry weapons. I just drive."

"Attitude like that has to cut down something fierce on offers."

"It's not attitude—it's principle. And I turn down more work than I take."

"This one's sweet."

Briefly, he told Driver about the score. One of those rich communities north of Phoenix, seven-hour drive, acre upon acre of half-a-mill homes like rabbit warrens, crowding out the desert's cactus. Then, writing something on a piece of paper, he pushed it across the table with two fingers. Driver remembered car salesmen doing that. People were so goddamned stupid. Who with any kind of pride, any sense of self, would go along with that? What kind of fool would even put up with it?

"This is a joke, right?" Driver said.

"You don't want to participate, don't want a cut, there it is. Fee for service. Keep it simple."

Driver stood. "Sorry to have wasted your time."

"Add a zero to it," he said.

"Add three."

"No one's that good."

Driver shrugged. "Plenty of drivers out there. Take your pick."

"I think I have." He held up his empty glass. "Four on the team, we split five ways. Two shares for me, one for each of the rest of you. Done?"

Driver nodded.

Just as the alto sax jumped on the tune's tailgate for a long, slow ride.

HE WASN'T SUPPOSED to have the money. He wasn't supposed to be a part of it at all. And he ought to be back at work doing double-eights and turnarounds. Jimmie, his agent, probably had a stack of calls for him. Not to mention the shoot he was supposed to be working on. The sequences didn't make much sense to him, but they rarely did. He never saw scripts; suspected the sequences wouldn't make a lot more sense to the audience. But they had flash aplenty. Meanwhile all he had to do was show up, hit the mark, do the trick. "Deliver the goods," as Jimmie put it. And he always did.

That Italian guy with all the forehead creases and warts was on the shoot, starring. Driver didn't go to movies and could never remember his name, but he'd worked with him a couple of times before. Always brought his coffeemaker with him, slammed espressos the whole day like cough drops. Sometimes his mother showed up and got escorted around like she was queen.

So here he was.

The score'd been set for nine that morning, just after opening. Seemed ages ago now. Four in the crew. Cook who'd put it together. New muscle up from Houston by the name of Strong. The girl, Blanche. Him driving, of course. They'd pulled out of L.A. at midnight. Blanche would grab everyone's attention while Cook and Strong moved in.

Driver'd been out three days before to get a car. He always picked his own car. The cars weren't stolen, which was the first mistake people made, pros and amateurs alike. Instead, he bought them off small lots. You looked for something bland, something that would fade into the background. But you also wanted a ride that could get up on its rear wheels and paw air if you needed it to. Himself, he had a preference for older Buicks, mid-range, some shade of brown or gray, but he wasn't locked in. This time what he found was a ten-year old Dodge. You could run this thing into the side of a tank and not dent it. Drop anvils on it, they'd bounce off. But when he turned the motor over, it was like this honey was just clearing its throat, getting ready to talk.

"Got a back seat for it?" he asked the salesman who'd gone along on the test drive. You didn't have to push the car, just run it through its paces. See how it cornered, if its center stayed put when you accelerated, slowed, cut in or out. Most of all, listen. There was a little too much play in the transmission for his taste. Clutch needed to come up some. And it pulled to the right. But otherwise it was about as perfect as he had any right to expect. Back at the lot, he crawled underneath to be sure the carriage was straight, axles and ties in good shape. Then asked about the back seat.

"We can find one."

He paid the man cash and drove it off the lot to one of several garages he used. They'd give it the works, new tires, oil and lube, new belts and hoses, a tune-up, then store it, where it would be out of sight till he picked it up for the job.

Next day, his call was at six a.m., which in Hollywoodese translated to show up around eight, nine. Guy working second unit held out for a quick take (why wouldn't he, that's what he got paid for) but Driver insisted on a trial run. Buggy they gave him was a white-over-aqua '58 Chevy. Looked cherry, but it drove like a goddamned mango. First run, he missed the last mark by half a yard. Good enough, the second-unit guy said. Not for me, Driver told him. Man, second-unit came back, this is what? two minutes of a film that lasts almost two hours? That rocked! Plenty of drivers out there, Driver told him. Call the union.

Second run went like a song. Driver gave himself a little more time to get up to speed, hit the ramp to go up on two wheels as he sailed through the alley, came back down onto four and into a moonshiner's reverse to face the way he'd come. The ramp would be erased in editing, and the alley would look a lot longer than it was.

The crew applauded.

He had one other scene blocked for the day, a simple run against traffic down an interstate. By the time the crew finished setting up, always the hardest part, it was almost one. Driver nailed it on the first run. Two-twenty-three, and the rest of the day belonged to him.

He caught a double-header of Mexican movies out on Pico, downed a couple of slow beers at a bar nearby making polite conversation with the guy on the next stool, then had dinner at the Salvadoran restaurant up the street from his crib, rice cooked with shrimp and chicken, fat tortillas with that great bean dip they do, sliced cucumbers and tomatoes.

By then he'd killed most of the evening, which is pretty much what he did when he wasn't working one job or the other. But even after a bath and half a glass of scotch he couldn't get to sleep. Should have paid attention then. Life sends us messages all the time, then sits laughing over how we're not gonna be able to figure them out.

So at three a.m. he's looking out the window at the loading dock across the street wondering if the crew over there, hauling stuff out of the warehouse and tucking it away in various trucks, is legal. Probably not. No further activity on the dock, no job boss, a certain furtiveness. Maybe he should heat things up, call the police, watch while it got more interesting. But he doesn't.

Around five, he pulled on jeans and an old sweatshirt and went out for breakfast at the Greek's.

THINGS START GOING wrong on a job, sometimes it starts so subtly you don't see it at first. Other times, it's all dominoes and fireworks.

This was somewhere in between.

Sitting in the Dodge pretending to read a newspaper, Driver watched the others enter. There'd been a small line waiting outside the door, five or six people. He could see them all through the blinds. Blanche chatting with the security guard just inside the door. Other two looking around, at the point of putting guns in the mix. Everyone still smiling, for now.

Driver also watched:

An old man sitting on the low brick wall across from the storefront, knees stuck up like a grasshopper's, struggling to get his breath;

Two kids, twelve or so, skateboarding down the sidewalk opposite;

The usual pack of suit-and-dress people heading for work clutching briefcases and shoulder bags, looking tired already;

An attractive, well-dressed woman perhaps forty years old walking a boxer from both sides of whose mouth strings of gluey saliva hung;

A muscular Latino offloading crates of vegetables from his double-parked pickup to a Middle Eastern restaurant down the block;

A Chevy in the narrow alley three storefronts down.

That one brought him up short. It was like looking in a mirror. Car sitting there, driver inside, eyes moving right to left, up, down. Didn't fit the scene at all. Absolutely no reason for that car to be where it was.

Then sudden motion inside caught his attention—everything happened fast, much of it he'd put together later—and Driver saw the backup guy, Strong, turn toward Blanche, lips moving. Watched him go down as she drew and fired before hitting the floor as though she'd been shot herself. Cook, the guy who'd put it all together, had begun firing in her direction.

He was still thinking *What the fuck?* when Blanche came barreling out with the bag of money and threw it onto the new back seat.

Drive!

Drive he did, pulling out in a brake-accelerator skid between a Fed Ex truck and a Volvo with a couple dozen dolls on the shelf by the rear windshield and a license plate that read *Earthship2*, not at all surprised to find the Chevy wheeling in behind him as he watched Earthship2 crash-land into the sidewalk bins of a secondhand book-and-records store.

Air would be thin there for Earthship2, the new world's natives hostile.

The Chevy stayed with them for a long time—the guy was that good—as Blanche sat beside him hauling money by the handful out of the gym bag, shaking her head and going, Shit! Shit!

The suburbs saved them, just as they saved so many others from the city's awful influence. Finding his way to the subdivision he had scouted earlier, Driver barreled onto a quiet residential street, tapping the brakes once, again, then again, so that by the time he reached the speed trap he was cruising a steady twenty-five. Not knowing the area and not wanting to lose them, the Chevy had come charging in. Driver watched in the rear view mirror as local cops pulled it over. Squad pulled up at an angle behind, motorcycle mountie in front. Guys would be telling this story back at the station for weeks.

Shit, Blanche said beside me. Lot more money here than there ought to be. Has to be close to a quarter of a million. Shit!

"I'M GONNA RUN across and grab something to eat," Blanche said. "I saw a Pizza Hut over there and I'm starved. Sausage and extra cheese okay?"

"Sure," he said, standing near the door, by one of those picture windows on aluminum tracks that all motels seems to have. The lower left corner had sprung out of the frame and he could feel warm air from outside pouring in. They were in a second-floor room facing front, with only the balcony, stairway and twenty yards or so of parking lot between them and the interstate. The motel itself had three separate exits. One ramp onto the interstate was off the intersection beyond the parking lot. Another was just up the street.

Had to be Blanche, of course. No other way the Chevy was down there in the parking lot.

She'd taken a brush out of her purse and started into the bathroom.

He heard her say "What—"

Then the dull boom of the shotgun.

Driver went in around Blanche's body, saw the man in the window, then slipped in blood and slammed into the shower stall, shattering the glass door and ripping his arm open. The man still struggled to free himself. But now he was lifting the gun again and swinging it towards Driver, who, without thinking, picked up a piece of the jagged glass and threw. It hit the man full on in the forehead. Pink flesh flowered there, blood poured into the man's eyes, and he dropped the shotgun. Driver saw the razor by the sink. He used it.

The other one was doing his best to kick the door in. That's what Driver had been hearing all along without realizing what it was, that dull drumming sound. He broke through just as Driver came back into the room—just in time for the shotgun's second load. Thing was maybe twenty inches long and it kicked like a son of a bitch, doing more damage to his arm. Driver could see flesh and muscle and bone in there.

Not that he was complaining, mind you.

FROM INSIDE HE heard the bleating of a terminally wounded saxophone. Doc had ideas about music that were different from most people's.

"Been a while," Driver said when the door opened to a nose like a bloated mushroom, poached eyes.

Doc stood there blankly. The sax went on bleating behind him. He glanced back that way, and for a moment Driver thought he might yell over his shoulder for it to shut up.

"No one plays like that anymore," Doc said with a sigh.

He looked down then, for what seemed a long time. "You're dripping on my welcome mat."

"You don't have a welcome mat."

"Used to. Then people somehow started getting the notion I meant it. . . . You're selling blood, I don't need any."

"*I* will, if you don't let me in."

Doc backed off, gap in the door widening. Man had been living in a garage when he and Driver first met, more years ago than either of them wanted to think about. Here he was, still living in a garage. Bigger one, though; Driver'd give him that. Doc had spent half a lifetime dispensing marginal drugs to the Hollywood crowd before he got shut down. Had a mansion up in the Hills, people said, so many rooms no one ever knew who was living there. People would wander up a stairwell during a party and not show up again for days.

"Have a taste?" Doc asked, pouring from a half-gallon urn of drugstore-brand bourbon.

"Why not?" If things went the way he hoped, he'd need it. If not, he'd need it even more. "Cheers," he said. Doc had all but filled a glass so bleary it might have been smeared with dirty Vaseline.

"That arm doesn't look so good."

"You think?"

"You want, I could have a look at it."

"You sure?"

"Please," he said. "Let me help. Let me be of use to someone again, just this once."

He scurried about gathering things. Driver watched closely. Some of the things he gathered were a little scary.

"Can't tell you how much I miss it," Doc said. "Medicine was the great love of my life. Never had another woman, never needed one. Been a while, though, like you say. Sure hope I remember how."

Rotted teeth broke into a smile.

"Relax, young man," he said, pushing Driver into a chair and swiveling a cheap desk lamp toward him. "Just having my fun. Just kidding." The bulb flickered, failed, came back when Doc thumped it. Taking a healthy swig himself, he handed Driver the half-gallon of bourbon.

"Have a few more hits off this, boy. Chances are you'll need them. Maybe we both will, before this is over. You ready?"

NOTHING IN THE car to lead him anywhere. He'd have been surprised if there were. Clean as a parched bone.

He had no way of running down the registration. Even if he had, it would almost certainly turn out to be faked.

Okay.

When the heavyweights didn't come back, whoever had sent them, whatever heads and bosses were up there above the whole thing, they'd would start looking for the car. Driver figured the best thing he could do was move the Chevy, stow it where it would be hard but not *too* hard to find, hang out and wait.

So for two days, arm aching like a son of a bitch every moment of every minute of every hour, imaginary knives slitting it from shoulder to wrist again and again, Driver sat across from the mall where he'd parked the Chevy. He forced himself to use the arm, even for the chi-chi coffee he bought, $3.68 a cup, at the open stand just inside the mall's east entrance. This was in Scottsdale, back towards Phoenix proper, a high-end suburb where each community had its own walls, and where stores in malls tended toward a Neiman-Marcus/Williams-Sonoma axis. Sort of place a vintage car like the Chevy wouldn't seem out of place. But Driver'd parked it on the lot's outer edge in the sketchy shade of a couple of palo verdes to make it easier to spot.

Not that it much mattered at this point, but he kept running things down in his head.

Cook had set them all up, of course. Driver'd seen Strong, go down— for good, to every appearance. Maybe Strong had been part of the set-up, maybe just a pawn in Cook's game. Blanche he wasn't sure about.

She could have been in from the first, but it didn't feel that way. Maybe she was only looking out for herself, keeping options open, trying to find her way out of the corner she and Driver had been shoved into. Far as he knew, Cook was still a player. No way Cook had the weight or stones for those guys in the Chevy, though. So he had to be fronting.

Making the question: Who was likely to show?

Any minute a car could pull up with goombahs inside.

Or maybe, just maybe, the bosses would insist, the way it sometimes worked, that Cook clean up after himself.

Nine-forty a.m. on the third day, every breeze in the state gone severely south and blacktop already blistering, arm hanging off his shoulder like a hot anvil, Driver thought: *Okay then, Plan B.* He watched Cook in a Crown Vic circle twice on the outer ring and pull into the lot just past the Chevy. Watched him get out, look around, amble toward the parked car, key in hand. Cook opened the driver's side, slid in. Soon he emerged, went around back and popped the trunk, leaned in.

Then, suddenly, he straightened and started to turn.

Driver was there.

"Shotgun's not much good anymore," he said. "Blanche isn't, either. But I thought a few props might help you remember what went down, what you're responsible for."

He had Cook in a choke hold he'd picked up on breaks from a stunt man he worked with on a Jackie Chan movie.

"Hey, relax. Guy I learned this from told me the hold's absolutely safe on a short-term basis," he said. "After four minutes, the brain starts shutting down, but up till then—"

Loosening his hold, he let Cook drop to the ground. Cook's tongue was extended and he wasn't breathing. A certain blueness to the skin. Tiny stars of burst blood vessels about the face.

"Always a chance I didn't get it quite right, of course. And it has been a while."

Driver took Cook's wallet, nothing much of use or note there, then went to the Crown Vic to toss that. A clutch of gas-station receipts jammed into the glove compartment, all of them from the downtown area, 7th Street, McDowell, Central. Four or five pages of scrawled directions to various spots in and around Phoenix, mostly unreadable. An Arizona roadmap. A sheaf of coupons bound together with a rubber band:

```
NINO'S PIZZA
(RESTAURANT IN BACK)

719 E. Lynwood
(480) 258-1433
```

From a phonebooth, Driver called the number on the coupons. The phone rang and rang—after all, it was still early. Whoever answered was adamant, as adamant as one could be in dodgy English, that Nino's was not open, that he would please have to call back after eleven.

"I could do that," Driver said, "but I don't think your boss will be happy waiting that long. Why don't you go tell him I've taken over for Cook."

Shortly a heavy, chesty voice came on.

"Nino." Probably couldn't spell it, but he pronounced it with authority.

"I have something of yours."

"Yeah, well, lots of people do. I got a lot of stuff. You have a name, too?"

"I do. Just as soon keep it."

"Whatever you say. I don't need no more names. What's this about Cook?"

"Wanted to let you know he's now keeping company with Strong and Blanche. Not to mention the goons you sent to a certain Motel 6."

Driver could hear the man breathing there at the end of the line.

"You some kind of fuckin' army?"

"I drive. That's what I do. All I do."

"Have to tell you, it's sounding like sometimes you might give a little extra value for the money, you know what I mean?"

"People make deals, they need to stick to them."

"That's what my old man always said. Been known to repeat it a few times myself."

"I haven't counted, but Blanche told me there was something like two hundred grand."

"And you're telling me this why?"

"It's your money. You say the word, it could be at your back door within the hour. But once it shows, we're even, right? That's the deal. You forget Cook, the goons. You forget all of it. No one steps up to me a week from now with your regards."

"Hey. I can live with that."

SIX A.M., FIRST light of dawn, like the world was stitching itself back together out there, recreating itself as he looked on. Blink, and the warehouse across the way was back. Blink again, the city loomed in the distance, like a ship coming into port. Half a dozen nervous birds skittered from ragged tree to ragged tree. Cars idled at curbside, took on human freight, pulled away.

Streets and highways filling.

Driver sat in his apartment sipping Scotch from the only glass he'd kept. The Scotch was Buchanan's, a mid-range blend. Not bad at all. Big seller among Latinos. Forties swing played on a cheap radio beside him. There was no phone, nothing of value, no furniture beside what came with the apartment. Clothes, razor, money and other essentials stayed in a duffel bag by the door.

A good car waited in the parking lot.

Sooner or later they'd come after him, of course, despite Nino's assurances. It was only a matter of time. Sooner or later Nino, money securely in hand, would get around to thinking how the bosses couldn't let this go—how they couldn't let it get out that hired help had brought them to heel.

Probably Nino had known that from the first. Driver, too.

So sky might fall, or ground rear up. If word failed to issue from Nino, bosses would send it down: Take care of this. Or it would rise from young enforcers looking to make themselves: I'll take care of this. One or the other.

Driver looked out on interstate, balcony, parking lot. Poured the last of the Buchanan's into his last glass. Guests soon, no doubt about it.

When Fire Knew My Name

COLD, DRIVING WEATHER like this always brought them out.

It had been there in early morning, a presence, a threat, a promise, and by seven had honed itself to a cleaverlike edge on the strop of wind. From my window on the fifth floor I listened to the schlep-schlep-schlep of that edge on the strop and watched as day congealed and the blade began to slice away at the city.

They emerged on their canes and crutches, in wheelchairs, tottering on artificial and makeshift limbs or balanced like flat-bottomed urns on low carts, pulling themselves along with gloved hands. At these times there is an expression on their faces that's difficult to describe. Pain, yes—but within it, at the core, the thing that pain comes wrapped around, a kind of joyfulness, I think.

Others, those to whom the world belonged, walked with heads down, swaddled in scarves and layers of wool and heavy caps. But the survivors tore open their own shabby coats and raised faces to the sky, threw out their arms to embrace it all: this wind, this blade, this impossible city.

"Don't tell me. The fire brigade's out." Somehow or another, originating in the punch line of a joke, I'm sure, that had become our name for them. Sandra stood in the doorway arch whose frame evoked both Chinese calligraphy and *pi* with sheet and blanket wrapped about her, a human teepee. Her hair, so blond it was almost white, had begun growing back in. It poked out a quarter-inch or so all around and she was convinced she looked like a dandelion. "Shut the shockin' window before your nose falls off."

"Yeah, and I've only got *one* of those."

In college, as was the fad for a couple of years, she'd had an ear removed. Half the people in the city her age were walking around with newly grown ones, but that wasn't Sandra's style. She started something, she stayed with it.

"If I shut the window, it frosts over and I can't see out."

"What—they look different this time?"

But of course they never did. They were as generic and predictable as spring, as the run of our daily lives, the news and entertainment piped in to us, what we said to one another. I shut the window. Wind howled as though in complaint and shook the pane fiercely with both hands.

"Breakfast?"

"I'd planned on fishes, but we're fresh out of loaves."

"The cupboard was bare."

"In a word."

"Not even a bone."

"A few exoskeletons, but I don't think those count."

Sandra and wrappings sank into one of the chairs. "I was dreaming," she told me. "Standing on the street looking up at a billboard." With one hand she sketched its cadence, form and line breaks on air. "We're almost done/ World finished soon/ Thank you for your patience/ B&D Construction.

"I'm standing there and I have this warm feeling in my stomach. I realize that for months, as cold winds blew in across bare plains to the east, I've been coming out each morning to admire new buildings that appear overnight, to be among the first to stroll new plazas, arcades, explore tiny parks. I'm tremendously proud of my city, what it's becoming.

"But there's also, it seems, a problem. When I return to my apartment, six brutally handsome young men in jeans, black T-shirts and low-slung toolbelts are waiting in the hall outside. They have to tear out my floor, they say. Possibly the walls as well. They'll know once they get started. But will I be able to stay here while you work? I ask them. Sure, no problem, the foreman says. Long as you don't need a floor or walls."

Rising, Sandra walked into the kitchen area and, ever the child of Famine parents, came out with a half-loaf of bread fetched from one hiding spot or another. I drew hot water, crumbled in tea leaves, and we fell to.

We'd been together almost four years. I'd gone with friends to HOUSE OF th'OUGHT and wound up sitting beside her. The House was another of those intermittent hot spots thronged with patrons for months when it opened, afterwards all but abandoned. Here great books were read aloud, in shifts, by professional readers. We were never able to agree on what was being read at the time. I remembered *Tristram Shandy*; Sandra insisted that by then Burning Cinder Person, the House's star reader and frequent subject of profiles in local papers during the House's brief heyday, was well into the 19th century.

(*In halflight she turns, murmuring, and I trace the scars along her back, by the shoulder blades. The sky splits open like a wound, and birds cough the sun into morning.*)

"So what's on for today?" she asked.

"Have to deliver my Cowboy tapes to Epoch-Z."

Cowboy's a figure so legendary that many claim he never existed. Supposedly he was the first of the great urban freedom fighters—some say the last as well—and went down in the seige of the markets. But street wisdom has it that Cowboy's still out there. He'd never been photographed except—possibly—for less than sixty seconds of blurry footage I'd caught years ago while filming deconstruction of the Skystop Building. One of the news channels was putting together a documentary on Cowboy. They'd learned of my tapes and offered enough money to keep me afloat, us afloat, for a year.

"What, you can't just shoot it to them? You're going outside? To someone's shockin' *office*?"

I shrugged. "They actually called up, on the phone. 'We may be on the bitter sharp edge, but we're also a little old-fashioned 'round here,' they tell me, 'in our own way.' Before I know it, I'm in a conference call with half a dozen vice presidents ranging in age between eighteen and eighteen-and-a-half. 'We like our people to have faces,' they tell me."

Jack London said to understand totalitarianism, picture a boot heel stamping on a human face—forever. Big business is soft Italian-leather loafers carressing that same face. However long and hard we espouse bohemian, alternative, libertarian, contrary lifestyles, we all live off big business, fleas on a dog. I tried to remember when heads of major corporations had begun showing up for work in pullovers and jeans. Revolution in America? Radical change? The country's very genius is its capacity to absorb anything, absolutely *anything*—to appropriate it, bear it on a flood into the mainstream, vitiate it.

"Anything I can pick up while I'm out?" I asked.

"Ginger would be good, for tonight's curry. Oh, and I guess some vegetables and rice. So there'll *be* a curry? Assuming I ever see you again."

"Think of it as an adventure," I said.

"Think of it as stupid," she said. "Not to mention the possibility of freezing nose, fingers and like wee appendages off."

"*Wee*? Did you say *wee*?" Reaching for a Scottish accent, which came out, inexplicably, Jamaican.

"Don't forget the ginger."

We say it together: "A Redemptionist never forgets."

THERE ON THE street away from river's edge, I encountered a more normal population—normal for this quarter of the city, that is. Fully half those out in the bite and slash hobbled along on feet with tendons fatally damaged by the police's standard interrogation technique: if they didn't like your answer, they stood on your foot and heaved you mightily backwards. Meanwhile uptown folk were paying clinics huge sums to have facial muscles injected with botulism. The bacteria paralyze the muscle and, in doing so, erase age lines. When these people talk, their eyebrows don't move but float cloudlike above their mouths, like dialog balloons in cartoons.

I began to penetrate the city's many folds and strata. I've always suspected it to be more laminate than veneer, thin sheets pressed close to form something of apparent substance, nothing, not even inferior materials, at its core.

At the corner of Market and Force, several hundred protestors converged in absolute silence on the plaza before City Hall. Riot police formed a human moat around the complex, beating sticks backhand against shields. The juxtaposition was uncanny. Protestors stood motionless looking across. Police beat at their shields. At some invisible cue the protestors withdrew as silently as they'd come.

At First and Desire, a small park had been set fire by the Children's Army. *We burn the bones they throw us*, a placard read. Children in red armbands stood alongside monitoring, making certain the fires did not spread. The fires were doing anything but, however. They were lowering, folding in upon themselves, benches turning to smolder. One of the children stepped forward into the park and gave a fingers-into-palm, come-to-me sign. *Incoming*, he shouted as half a dozen Molotov cocktails rained from windows of the high-rise project skirting the park.

Two blocks up, a crowd had gathered. They shouted encouragement, chanted, raised fists in the air. Leaning against the wall of a nearby credit union was a piece of cardboard cut from a heavy box and laboriously hand-lettered in cockeyed, backward-leaning block letters.

STREET FITING!

It was already over, though, the crowd dispersing, as I approached. One man lay broken and bleeding, body in the street, head on the curb as though on a pillow. I watched as his eyes went still. The other, the winner, wiped blood from *his* eyes and picked up the hat with the money. Then he walked to the sign, lifted it for a closer look, tucked it underarm. His now. Spoils.

The city I find when I come out into it, the one I'm a part of, is invisible to many. As though the city's gone belly up, as though this gray sky were an overturned stone. These are the forgotten people, the ones who don't matter, those ground down on the city's mill, used up, thrown beneath the wheels. Here there is neither history nor future, only a perpetual present tense of motion, hunger, need and momentary ease, a fire that consumes and goes on consuming, through whose flickering silent tongues sometimes we glimpse the shape, the form, the suggestion, of another reality, another world. A better one? Different, at least. And different is enough.

"Cowboy!" I cried out.

He stood at a street corner, buckskin fringe blowing in the breeze, looking a little confused when I approached him. We were at the dangerous border between uptown and down. Age lines crouched like homesteaders, deepset, at eyes and mouth. I took note of the missing ear.

"What's up?" I said. Like so many others, looking for guidance.

"What's ever up but more of the same? Just they practice new grimaces in the mirror is all, tell us more outrageous lies. *You* feel connected?"

No.

But had I ever?

"We have to keep changing. Dodging under, going over, scrambling. We can't let them get a hold, take us for granted."

"But you . . ."

Seeing the sudden sadness in his eyes, I understood. He was an icon. He couldn't change.

"Here's my ride," he said, stepping not into the city bus one would have thought he awaited but into an ancient VW bus. "Keep the faith?"

I watched him pull away.

Against the horizon the day still burned into life and burned steadily away, like alcohol, in a blue flame. No heat to any of it. What could a man do?

After a moment I snapped an ear plug off the tab and fit it in as I started walking again along the street, past crews of workers tearing up streets, crews of workers rebuilding them. You never know what you'll get, of course, that's part of the deal, but this was okay. *We'll Meet Again in Glory*. I watched my breath go out in plumes with each step.

Glory was the next town over.

Get Along Home

IT WON'T BE long.

I nodded.

Sorry to take you away.

No problem. I told you I'd be here.

I always knew you would.

A nurse practitioner stepped into the room. As she did so, lighting came up perceptibly, brightening around our small island of bed, table, chair. Is there anything you need? she asked. Her signing was rapid, assured; until then I'd not been conscious of signing, only that we were speaking, speaking the way it seemed we'd always spoken. I'd slipped back into it so naturally, after all these years.

No, but thank you, Tish said. You're so kind.

And to me, once the nurse had withdrawn: There's so much I have to tell you, to ask you.

I nodded. A pigeon lit on the sill outside. Sad looking bird. It staggered on its way to the window, its beak bent back on itself when it pecked at the window. But a bird nonetheless. Most of the others were extinct. How long since I'd even seen one?

Have you been happy? she asked.

Yes.

And are you now?

Most days, I think.

You always had good answers, love.

The pigeon's eye was an orange jewel. It bobbed its head up and down, side to side in that curious stitch they have, trying to understand. Knew it should be wary, wasn't sure of just what.

Everything.

We never get very far from where we start, do we?

That said, her hand fell back exhausted onto the sheet. The word *breathless* came to me.

It's what they call in sports a broken-field run, I told her. They all know where you're headed, but there's that whole field between here and there. You keep moving, keep dodging. Everything's footwork, evasion, misdirection.

They?

The opposition. The visiting team.

She sat looking out at the pigeon.

I hate to ask this, but. . . .

Seeing where her eyes went, I said: It's all right. I arranged her gown about her, helped her onto the bed pan. Flesh on hips and stomach had collapsed, folding in on itself like a tent being taken down. She seemed almost weightless. Breasts, too, hung limp and deflated. Our selves, our identities, are so linked to sexuality. When we no longer have that, in a sense I suppose we become something else.

Once I had wanted this woman so badly. And once this body, like my own, ached just to be wanted. Where do all those feelings go? Into some ozone layer, maybe, out of sight and mind. Forever building up, protecting us quietly.

She turned her face to the wall, eyes unblinking, as I cleaned her.

I brought this for you, I said afterwards.

She held up the clear disk, turning it side to side, watching me through it.

A game I designed. I worked on it a long time. The producers think it's a sure hit.

Her eyes said: Tell me about it.

A man is on his way home from work. Everything goes wrong. He doesn't have exact change, the subway founders, a trio of terrible musicians comes aboard his car. Finally he exits, and comes up into a part of the city he can't recognize at all. He begins walking. Nothing is familiar. He's surrounded by whores in red boots, guys without bottom halves who cruise the city on plywood rafts atop roller skates, twitchy teens stepping off curbs to meet cars and glancing up every four seconds to rooftops, lawyers who've set up offices on the street like lemonade stands, an Islamic Mormon shepherding his flock of wives down towards the harbor. The goal's to get him home.

I hope it does well for you.

Me too. I've a lot of time invested.

Years ago, she said after a moment, I knew a man who was going to be a painter.

Yes, I said. I knew him too.

She nodded, and her eyes went to the window. The pigeon was gone. Rectangle full of darkening sky.

Maybe you should rest now.

Okay.

There are some things I need to take care of. I'll be back later.

Smiling, she closed her eyes. I was almost to the door when I heard her knock on the bedside table, and turned.

"I thought this would be more interesting," she said. From such long disuse and from the damage done, her voice was a poor engine. She had to repeat what she'd said before I understood. Many years had passed since last I heard it, but the disappointment in her voice was something I knew well.

As I stepped into the hall, the nurse practitioner rose from a molded plastic chair. She held one of those heavily waxed packages of juice with a midget straw. Her name tag was a simple rectangle: Carson.

"Do you have any questions?"

I shook my head.

"You do understand, I hope: It wasn't a decision she made lightly."

"To die, you mean."

"We all die, Mr. Decker."

"Most of us for reason, though."

"She has reasons. Some of them we can understand, a lot we never will. Not that it matters."

"That sounds perilously close to mysticism, Ms. Carson."

"We don't much pretend to science here. We're more like . . . I don't know . . . wilderness guides, maybe. Helpmates."

She finished her drink and dropped the package into a reclamation bin. With some surprise I realized that we'd been speaking aloud. I had resurfaced, I was back in the world.

"She never could stand decisions being made for her. You know that better than anyone. And it explains a lot, for those of us who need explanations."

"One could look at it that way. Or as easily consider it little more than another expression of massive ego. Just another performance."

Like the time she'd crawled, naked and without language, out of the ice sculpture of a mammoth that artisans had spent eighteen hours carving. Or the way, years back, back when she spoke, she'd sit on stage and slit her skin with razors while reading aloud from the daily newspaper.

"It won't be long, Mr. Decker. You're leaving?"

I nodded.

"I'll call you, if you'd like."

I thanked her and gave her my number. Like the pigeon, I left. Soon I'd be extinct, too. We all would. Meanwhile the goal was to get me home. I had a good chance of making it.

Blue Yonders

I STOOD AND watched as the dogs, our dogs, swept down the hill into battle, a thrilling sight however many times one has seen it. Their own, emerging from runnels and arroyos, appeared instantly to meet ours, as if somehow materialized from the ground itself. Soon the field was a mass of leaping, tumbling, snapping, tearing bodies. Some of the dogs went straight for the throat; others struck at haunches or flanks to maim and disable, to bring their opponents down quickly, then moved on. Wave after wave drove down from the trees, off the horizon cradled atop this hill. Rank after rank rose from the low ground to meet them. The dogs went about their work in absolute silence.

Eventually, as always it must be, it was over. Their general stood now on the hill across from mine. As I walked down into the valley, as I lifted my eyes, he lowered his. We nodded to one another.

Unlike the dogs, we, the people of my village, did not go silently about our business, but called out encouragement and direction to one another over their bodies, spoke quietly, commented, even laughed from time to time, as we cleared the field. Men hoisted the bodies chest-high and laid them out on carts and litters; women followed, scooping up severed limbs and entrails in wooden shovels; small children pulled travoises or carried water about to workers. The clearing took, as always it does, many hours, at the end of which we were in equal parts exhausted, exhilarated.

In the village, afterwards, there was feasting. Fresh meat grilled on skewers over slow fires of cypress and fig, fresh meat stewed with turnips and a variety of other roots in clay pots over those same fires, fresh meat chopped with purple and green peppers, wrapped in palm leaves and buried in the coals. Savory smoke rolled everywhere, eyes and mouths watered. Bal strummed the single string of his banjer as Ariana improvised songs celebrating our triumph, celebrating, too, each of the dogs that had given its life for us. At one point Bal, taken up with the song, strummed so fiercely that the string broke. As he set about preparing another, this being a process that required some time, Ariana continued a capella her praise of the dogs, of their courage and devotion: praise of the flesh that, having so ably and expertly defended us, now enriched us.

Later along still, when feasting and songs were over and only dregs of sweet-potato wine remained asludge in the bellies of the barrels, three young women sat crosslegged outside my tent, speaking in low whispers among themselves. Twelve to fourteen summers they had seen, perhaps a dozen such great wars. Baskets of fruit ripe like themselves sat beside these women, other baskets filled with stones polished round and smooth by the river, sacred mud still clinging to them. Taking a bite from each of the fruits, I set them in a line before the woman I'd chosen and circled her with stones. The others departed to return to their families, their parents, brothers; to await the next deliverance.

Her name, she told me, was Chai. Because she came from another village, it was a name I had not heard before, the C turning, almost before one heard it, into an S on her lips. She smiled then took in her breath quickly when I entered and broke her, and afterwards, in her sleep, spoke quietly to herself or perhaps to some dream companion, drawing up her knees like a child.

A short night it was, and the whole of it I lay there alongside Chai, my wife. Outside, the moon shone and rippled like a pool of white water. Towards dawn a plaintive wind blew up from the lowlands. In their corrals, in their sleep, the new dogs moaned and tossed restlessly about, hungry for glory.

Stepping Away from the Stone

HE LEFT HER there on the litter by her parent's trunk, knowing she'd need to be alone now. He went out into the other room and sat by the open door sipping at the pod of warm pulp she'd set out for him before. It was dark outside, gray turning relentlessly over inside itself, almost morning. In the open square just beyond the door a tree moved several steps to the right, into a patch of dull light, and resettled itself with something like a sigh sounding in its leaves. The leaves were perfectly rectangular, curling towards midline and tip like a tongue.

Much of his life, he knew, would be spent contemplating what had just taken place. But for now, newly set adrift on his future, he took refuge in the past, in his own memories and those of his parents.

A limitless white ceiling, the only world he yet had. The voices that came to him there, like a rain one heard—voices that came to him still sometimes, unbidden.

A crimson, restless sea.

Fields of migrating grain.

The husk of his parent's body just before he returned it to the trees.

The tree moved again, to the left this time, and settled back. He thought how so much of their lives, fiber for clothing, materials for shelter, medicines, even basic sustenance, came from the trees.

Then she emerged from the back room.

They sat together in the doorway, soles of their feet pressed against one another. He passed the pod and she drank. Pulp, from the tree.

The world looks no different, she signed.

No.

But it is. I thank you for your choice, for my freedom.

He signed that it was of no import and passed the pod to her again. Lowering her head, she drank. Lifting the pod, he drank. Light pushed gently at the backside of gray beyond the door. The tree shifted again, into whatever tatters remained of darkness.

She drank off the last of the liquor, gathering final shreds of pulp onto her smaller thumb and offering it to him.

There is more, she signed. He assented, and she went to draw another podful from the gourd as, waiting, he witnessed morning's arrival. Slow eddies gave way to pools of silver above the trees; then, riding from its center, there was sudden light. Around them the low, wordless moan of the trees.

And with the morning, morning's chill.

She closed the door and sat beside him again, soles of her feet against his. He watched her across this chasm, you could bridge it with an out-reached hand but no one ever would, her lidless eyes, pale blue skin.

Passing the pod from hand to hand, they drank. Unseen light went on growing outside, reclaiming its world. A general sense of increment, augmentation. A growing sense of loss.

These walls, he signed. That shut us away?

He sat watching one. Pale white like the pith of plants rising from still water, like every wall he had ever seen.

There could be openings, he signed. Eyes in the walls. Out of those eyes we would continue as part of the world, never again be shut away from it. Those eyes would be formed of some material one could see through.

But there is nothing like that, she signed, nothing one can see through.

He assented. Then stood to sign:

There is a stone, a tree. Man waits. In due time, he steps away from the stone.

Woman waits too, she signed. In due time, she steps away from the tree.

He took from her the bundle she offered. Tied with a single white rib-bon, it was almost weightless.

Nothing left but the world now, he thought as he went out the door. All this light. All this future he carried with him. The new memories he would have.

Flagging a barge nestwards, he sat on narrow branches among others rushing to or from. At length as they watched, dark began to gather, coming not from the sky, not as descent, but pooling up from the ground like oil: tree and stone united.

Nested, he pulled loose the ribbon tie about the bundle she'd given him. Light as thistledown it unscrolled, barely there at all, floor visible beneath as through water.

Some material one could see through.

Her face fell lightly, transparently, almost weightless, against his hand. Vacant eye slots looking up.

As dark fell then, lifting this precious skin to his lips, he began to eat, began to remember.

Second Thoughts

I WAS WAKENED by a polite, quiet coughing in the front room. I crawled across the Murphy bed, pushed the door open and looked out. On the sofa sat a small, pale man. His legs were crossed and he stared silently out, watching as boats pulled themselves slowly down the river calling to one another through the fog. Lights entered by the same window. They flared in dark eyes, turned to shadow, dropped onto a white shirt. His hair was a startling black, cheekbones high, face narrow as a plank.

He turned his head slowly towards me. "What can I do to make you believe that I'm wholly sincere?" he said. It was then that I recognized him: this was Artaud.

I got out of bed, without speaking went to the desk for a pen and paper, put them before him.

"You don't know what it's like," he said. "You come out of it and you can't find yourself. Something is irretrievably lost."

Unthinkingly he began to draw on the paper, sketchy gray lines tumbling into patches of black scribble. Faces of those he knew, perhaps, devil masks, plugs of matter pulled from deep within the world's core.

I nodded and moved to switch on a small electric lamp beside him. He pulled himself up straight in the chair, alarmed. I stepped back. Another boat came into view in the window.

"'Very little is needed to destroy a man; he needs only the conviction that his work is useless,'" I said.

Outside, a car stopped in the street opposite and its headlights went off. There was the sound of doors closing, laughter, a young man and woman. Artaud listened intently, and only when their voices vanished into the house did he turn back, to stare down at the paper on his lap.

Everything he had, everything he was, strained now towards the external world that lay outside himself, I felt: strained, and fell short.

On my way back to the bedroom I turned on the radio. Softly, so neighbors would not be bothered. Porter Waggoner was singing about "The Cold Hard Facts of Life." My visitor turned his head towards the radio and the light from outside hung on the bones of his face, making his cheeks look cavernous, hollow, reminding me of Yeats: "and took a mess of shadows for its meat."

Anne was four days gone. Slow glide along the ridge of mountain rimming our city at six in the morning, spilling over into America. When she told me she was leaving, I quoted Cavafy. Don't hope for new worlds or new seas, I told her. The way your life is ruined here in this small corner is the way it's ruined everywhere.

As I drifted back into sleep I realized another voice had joined that of my first visitor.

"Volition," said one.

"Guilt," said the other.

Antonin Artaud and Claude Eatherly were discussing the problem of conscience.

Christian

SOMETIMES HE IS there again, with the field burning around him, trees at the perimeter igniting one by one, flaring up like birthday candles. Sometimes it happens at night and he wakes in a pool of sweat. Sometimes he hears the pop-pop-pop of rifles in the distance set against the whoosh of trees igniting, sometimes it all takes place in silence. Sometimes, though not as often, it comes upon him by day.

THE CEILING IS so low that, legs spread and raised straight up, short as she is, her toenails scratch at it. Basically her home is a cardboard shipping case that's been stuccoed into some sort of permanence and place. Her toenails are long and slightly curved. He listens to this, listens to the scrape of the swayback bed against the wall as he pushes into her, hears the cry of hawkers in the street outside with their vegetables and rice, their bundles of lemongrass and herbs and seasoned rice tied with twine, their canvas bags of prawns and tiny crabs. She has not said a word the whole time, nor will she. She never does. Two infants stand on tiptoe in a crib made of green bamboo, watching, eyes white as boiled eggs.

HE GOT TO be known as Christian because once, upon completing an assignment, he stood for a moment with head down—as though in prayer, his back-up, an ill-dressed, illiterate young man of twenty or so, thought.

He was tired, nothing more, but the name stuck.

HE'S FIVE AND his father has taken him for ice cream. One of those late summer evenings that seem to go on forever. They sit outside, a low stone wall onto which Father has lifted him. City lights gleam behind. He can smell the sweet flowers at the base of the wall as insects bang into his ears and neck. I have spent my life leaving, his father says. A lifetime of giving things up. Leaving behind my class, my home, my country—my soul. Promise me you won't let the world to do to you what it has done to me. The boy has no idea what Father is talking about, of course. But dutifully he promises.

THE BARK AND roar of fireworks began. In his sixth-floor apartment through a rift between buildings off Third Avenue Christian watched them: spinning wheels, nebulae, immense palm trees of red and blue and green that sprouted, grew huge in an instant, and expired. Earlier, pigeons had been lined up like putti in the crannies of buildings and peering down from cornices. Now they were gone.

He'd been in New York for most of a week, since June 29th, living in an apartment sublet through an ad in the New York Review of Books. Its owner wished to evade the worst of the New York summer and spend these months, instead, on a beach in Massachusetts. He could have provided references, of course, but the heft of his check (drawn to an account he'd never again use) proved reference enough.

He found himself quite close by Gramercy Park, that odd bit of city real estate reserved for local homeowners and hotel guests, all of whom are in possession of keys. Meanwhile, outside, the flotsam of the city, its driftwood, washes by. From time to time these can be seen with faces pressed to the bars and locked gates.

In Chinatown the stores were filled with takeouts for hell. The Chinese burn paper imitations of things from this life to send with the newly dead into the other, things they will have need of there. Hell notes—false paper money—had always been available. But now the shops held shelf upon shelf of paper shirts, cars, make-up kits, evening slippers, cutlery, keys, armchairs, luggage, tea sets. Since his last visit, paper computers, cell phones and CD players had appeared as well—even a palm pilot or two. Like us, the dead must keep track of their appointments.

Christian had an appointment of his own. He was looking for a man named Shelley, a man who in public life, as a Washington lobbyist, wielded tremendous invisible power and who, in personal life, was enamored of anything perceived to be on the cultural cutting edge. Christian had spent his nights on roundabout tours of the Village, SoHo, NoHo, Tribeca, Park Slope, Queens. He'd witnessed klezmer played by an orchestra of kazoos of every size, exhibitions of toast sculpture and lawn ornaments, a theatrical improvisation in which the title on the marquee was left blank to be filled in after the performance, plays delivered with actors's backs turned to the audience, a one-man show featuring an old tin washtub in which the ice sculpture of a half-submerged, bright-green alligator slowly melted. Then, out in Williamsburg, in the basement of a Unitarian church, an extraordinary dance recital.

The curtain opened on a group of androgynous dancers in blue-green light. They lay, at first, motionless on the floor, and when they began to move, it was slowly, so slowly that one couldn't be sure there'd been movement at all. Something troubling, alien, even repulsive about it. They writhed and rolled and reached about in ways that had nothing to do with being human. They had become primitive organisms, sea-creatures just beginning to explore their surround, groping blindly towards food, reproduction, spinal columns, dry land, cliff dwellings, cities. All this conducted in absolute silence.

Christian carried those forms away with him. In doorways as he walked to the subway stop, past the train's window at Bedford Avenue and at Fulton Street, in dark recesses of stations and in creches passed once the train dove underground, those primordial creatures writhed still in their agony of becoming.

At Bergen they transferred. Just past Jay Street-Borough Hall, Christian moved onto the seat alongside Shelley.

HE LIVES IN Hoboken, New Jersey, but sometimes, remembering his father's stories, imagines himself in the old country, in a courtyard there. Smell of cabbage soup seeping down like a stain from upper floors, an old man seated in a kitchen chair outside one of the identical doors of the featureless block of apartments playing accordion. He's twelve. He waits out back by the trash bins. Soon enough she'll be along. She'll crouch low staring at him and after a while, still in a crouch, ease forward to the spillover about the bins, sniffing through it for food. For weeks he sat without moving against the far wall. Then began moving closer, inches each day. Eventually he got her to take a frankfurter (all he could raid from the refrigerator with some chance it might not be noticed) from his extended hand. She never came closer to him than that. She'd approach cautiously, take the food, and withdraw a yard or so to eat, watching him the whole time.

Sometimes other cats showed up there as well. They'd arch backs, turn sideways to make themselves appear larger, hiss, growl. But Gray wasn't like that. Half the size of most of them, scrawny and chronically undernourished, she never hesitated, never displayed. She simply, upon sight, rushed and tore into them. Most of her teeth were gone, probably from just such confrontations. But those other cats always fled.

Much of a year went by. He gained over a foot in height, a frosting of dark hair on his face, a voice he couldn't control. Gray gained weight; her coat began to look smooth and full. Then one day after school, as always, he went out to see her, carrying food he'd saved from his cafeteria lunch, and found something there by the bins that he didn't understand. He walked closer. It was an animal trap of some kind. And under its sharp jaws, in a pool of thick dark stuff, lay what looked like a rabbit foot.

He never saw Gray again. But he waited there for hours with his baseball bat until the trap's setter came to check. An older man from the apartments, who wore plaid pants and a yellow nylon shirt and kept licking his lips, and who smelled bad.

HE'D TRIED ON the good American life. It didn't fit.

The ideal world inside his parents' 18-inch TV had little to do with the real one he saw around him. Like a pinball he bounced from college to jungle back to college to advertising copywriter to teaching at a junior college. His country kept threatening war against largely TV-less countries. Its heroes turned from statesmen and creative artists to eighteen-year-old singers and movie actors of dubious talent.

Suddenly he had a wife, and this house in Dallas not far from Highland Park. Then one day as he left work on the way home he just kept driving. He'd called before he left; she was fixing meatloaf and mashed potatoes for dinner. Up around Plano, when the BMW ran out of gas, he got out and walked.

SHE WAS A liberal running for congress in proto-conservative Arizona and had the opposition running scared. She didn't think of herself as a liberal, far from it, but she had these peculiar notions, absolute equality, percentage taxation without breaks, open access to medical care, things like that, all of which made her suspect despite the fact that she'd served in the Air Force, a pilot no less, and been multiply decorated during the Gulf War. The good old boys who shepherded party and state just had no idea what to do with or about her. They ignored her as long as they could.

Way it works is, you get a message, usually by phone. You call back, they call back. Till finally there's a meeting somewhere and the job gets laid out.

Christian liked her from the first, as he watched from afar. The way she carried herself. Strands of gray that ran through her hair. The dark suit she wore that first time he saw her, almost like a man's, even to a kind of stylized necktie. He carried back the sound and sight of her laughter to his room at Motel 6. Next day he went to the library, the one downtown that looked like a ship under sail, and dug in.

"What the hell's this?" his runner asked three days later.

"Front money," Christian said.

"So—what? You're not fulfilling the contract?"

"Discretion's implicit. I'm discretioning."

"They won't like this."

Christian shrugged. His hand fell onto the runner's atop the table and gripped it hard.

"Take a message back for me. Tell them nothing happens to her."

"Just what the fuck's *your* problem?"

"Anything does—anything even starts to happen to her—first, I come after you. Then I take down the contractor. Then I go after the clients."

"You really think you can do that, man? There are too many of them."

"There always are."

Christian released his hand.

He put the runner down two weeks later, leaving him in the restroom of a $$$$ restaurant in Georgetown with credit cards fanned at his feet like a poker hand. The first contractor was found garroted on the butcher-block table in the house to the right of the congresswoman. It had been on the market for two months. A half-assembled rifle lay beside him. Days later, a body showed up in the pool of another house just down the street, at the intersection, rubber duck glued to the coarse hair and thick blood on its chest.

DOWNTOWN, LOOKING OVER at the spire of Westward Ho!, once Phoenix's luxury hotel and bustling with celebrities, now a retirement home, he sat as a herd of young children on a field trip broke around him, their adventure overseen by stale, sweet-smelling men in khaki slacks, print shirts and running shoes. The children all lugged backpacks. It would be a tough journey.

PP's, his father had called them. The privileged proletariat. Mottled pink cheeks, hair snipped to uniform height and perfect lines like their lawns, even the light in their eyes dialed down to a modest gleam. Nothing in the world, not giant rats nor pestilence nor the man stepping out of the alley with a broken bottle as you pass, was scarier than these folk.

Christian glanced at his watch. Almost one. The man he was looking for would be along shortly.

Long ago the Roseannes, Mariah Careys and George Bushes of this country had colonized imaginations, took them over entire. Hackneyed dreams have been driven like schrapnel into our beings and, lodged too close to vital organs, cannot be removed. Feudalism has been reinstated. The media live in the big house.

TWO MESSENGERS HAD been sent after him so far, two that he knew of, the first a shooter intending a single, clean takedown off the roof of a midtown garage (he'd caught the glint of the rifle barrel in a car window), the second a couple of guys who stepped up to him out of an alley downtown and wanted before doing their job to make sure he understood how tough they were and who moments later lay in the alley's mouth, participles eternally adangle, grammar forever uncorrected.

ELECTION NIGHT, CHRISTIAN sat up late, sipping brandy and levering Vienna sausages from cans with thumb and forefinger, clicking back and forth from an old movie to poll results. His candidate (and he smiled, thinking how this was the way he thought of her, this man who had never and would never vote) won by a narrow margin.

He supposed he must have been very drunk by the time final results were in. Vaguely, the next morning, he remembered standing before a mirror in conversation.

I won't try to explain my actions, he said . . . This has nothing to do with redemption . . . After a lifetime, one good act, even that one equivocal, it can't make much difference . . . She's a decent, honest woman. . . .

He remembered turning then from mirror to window, where rain ran down, bearing the world away.

SOMETIMES HE IS there again, with the field burning around him, trees at the perimeter igniting one by one, flaring up like birthday candles. Sometimes it happens at night and he wakes in a pool of sweat with the pop-pop-pop of rifles and the whoosh of trees still in his ears. Sometimes, though not as often, it comes upon him by day.

And this, too: one time, not far off, he steps from the cover of tall buildings into an open space, into sunlight, and looks up. There is no reason for the shadow he sees there before him. No tree or cloud, no tower, no plane. What I did, he thinks, was small, but good. He steps into the shadow and comes to a standstill there, smiling, waiting.

Concerto for Violence and Orchestra

TO THE MEMORY OF JEAN-PATRICK MANCHETTE

IT IS A beautiful fall day and he has driven nonstop, two days chewed down to the rind and the rind spit out, from New York. He should be tired, exhausted in fact, spent, but he isn't. Every few hours he stops for a meal, briefly trading the warm vinyl Volvo seat for one not unlike it in a string of Shoney's, Denny's and Union 76 truckstops. On the seat and the floorboard beside him are packets of water crackers, plugs of cheese, bottles of selzer and depleted carry-out cups of coffee, wasabi peas. In the old world he drove away from, tips of leaves had gone crimson, bright yellow and orange, gold. Now he is coming into the desert outside Phoenix, the nearest thing he ever had to a home. Crisp morning air rushes into open windows. He passes an ostrich farm, impossibly canting stacks of huge stone like primitive altars out among the low scrub and cholla, a burning car at roadside with no one nearby. On the radio a song he vaguely remembers from what he thinks of as Back Then plays. He is happy. Strangely, this has nothing to do with the fact that soon he will be dead or that within the past month he has killed four people.

PRYOR WAS THE one who told him about it. There were these small rooms behind the huge open basement area used for church dinners, summer Bible School, youth meetings, evenings of amateur entertainment where groups of teenagers blackened faces with burnt cork and donned peculiar hats for minstrel shows, nerdish young men in ill-fitting suits and top hats urged objects from thin air and underscored the tentativeness of it all by transforming silk handkerchiefs to doves, sponge balls to coins, and where the church's music director in his hairpiece trucked out again and again, relentlessly, his repertoire of pantomime skits: a man flying for the first time, a foreigner confronted for the first time by jello, a child on his first fishing trip forced to bait his own hook. (Is there something intrinsically funny about firsts?)

In the ceiling of one of those rooms was a small framed section, like a doorway. You could drag the table beneath, Pryor said, place a chair on the table, reach up and push the inset away. Then you could climb up in there. And if you kept going, always up, along stairways and ladders and catwalks, in and out of cramped crawlspaces, eventually you'd arrive at the steeple, where few before had ever ventured. A great secret, Pryor intimated. The whole climb was probably the equivalent of three floors at the most. But to Quentin's eyes and imagination then, the climb seemed vast, illimitable, and he felt as though he might be ascending into a different, perhaps even a better, world.

It would not take much, after all. For it to be a better world.

Pushing the door out of its frame and pulling up from the chair, legs flailing, Quentin found himself in a low chamber much like a closet turned on its side. He couldn't stand erect, but the far end of the chamber was unenclosed, and he passed through into an open, vaultlike space with a narrow walkway of bare boards nailed to beams. The nailheads were the size of dimes. Four yards or so further along, this walkway turned sharply right, fetching up rather soon at the base of a stairway steep and narrow as a ladder. The last few yards indeed *became* a ladder. Then he was there. Alone and far above the mundane, the ordinary, all those lives in their suits and cars and their cluttered houses with pot roasts cooking in ovens and laundry drying on lines out back. Quentin had seen *Around the World in Eighty Days* half a dozen times. This must be what it was like to go up in a balloon, float free, feel the ground surrender its claim on you. He was becoming David Niven.

Meanwhile he'd given no thought to Pryor, who seemed to have failed to follow, if indeed Pryor had begun at all.

Sunday School teacher Mr. Robert, however, had been giving them both thought. He'd only a quarter-hour past dismissed the boys, and now took note of their absence from services. So it was that, shortly after attaining his steeple, Quentin found himself being escorted down the aisle alongside Pryor and deposited in a front pew as Brother Douglas paused dramatically in his sermon, light fell like an accusing finger through stained-glass windows illustrating parables, and the entire congregation looked on.

He was caught that time, but never again.

The steeple became Quentin's special place. Just as other children spend hours and whole days of their lives sunk into books, board games or television, so Quentin spent his in the steeple, there by speaker horns that had taken the place of bells, sandwiches and a thermos of juice packed away in his school lunch box. Since of all things at his disposal his parents were least likely to miss one can of it among many, the sandwiches were generally Spam, which Quentin liked with mayonnaise and lots of pepper, sometimes sliced pickles. The bread was white, the juice that in name only, wholly innocent of fruit, rather some marvelous, alchemical compounding of concentrates, artificial flavors and Paracelsus knows what else.

Sometimes up there in the steeple Quentin would pull himself to the edge and lie prone, propping elbows at the correct angle and sighting along an imaginary rifle as Jenny Bulow, Doug Prather or the straggling Dowdy family climbed from cars and crossed the parking lot below.

Years later, half a world away and more than once, Quentin would find himself again in exactly that same position.

But this has nothing to do with his life now, he always insisted – to himself, for few others knew about it. That was another time, another place. Another person, you might as well say. Quentin came home from that undeclared war and its long aftermath an undeclared hero even to himself, and after much searching (*You have no college? You have to have college!*) took a job at Allied Beverage, where he still works. Where he worked until last month, at least. He hasn't been in, or called, and doubts they've held the position for him. It's not as though they'd have much difficulty finding someone to take up his slack: keep track of health-care benefits, paid time off, excused absences, time and attendance, IRAs. Holidays the company loaded employees up with discontinued lines, champagnes no one asked to the prom, odd bottled concoctions of such things as cranberry juice and vodka, lemonade and brandy, licorice-flavored liqueurs. After work they'd all be out in the parking lot stowing this stuff in trunks. It would follow them home, go about its unassuming existence on various shelves and in various cabinets till, months or years later, it got thrown out. The company made little more ado over throwing away its people.

HE PUSHED. RECENTLY there'd been rain, and enough water remained to bear the body away. But you couldn't see the water. It looked as though the body were sliding on its back, on its own momentum, along the canal. Further on, an oil slick broke into a sickly rainbow. Food wrappers, drink containers, condoms, beer cans and unidentifiable bits of clothing decorated the canal's edge. Down here one entered an elemental world, cement belly curved like a ship's hold, walls to either side as far as one could see. Jonah's whale, what Mars or the moon might look like, a landscape even more basic than that stretching for endless miles around the city. Out there, barren land and plants like something dredged from sea bottoms. He looked up. Air shimmered atop the canal's cement walls, half a dozen palm trees thrust shaggy heads into the sky. The body moved slowly away from him in absolute silence. Out a few yards, it hit deeper water, an imperceptible incline perhaps, and picked up speed, began to turn slowly round and round. Water had soaked into the fabric of the man's cheap blue suit and turned it purple. Blue dye spread out like a stain in the water beneath him. When he looked up again, two kids were there on the wall, peering over. Their eyes went back and forth from the body to him. He waved.

HE'D PICKED UP a new car nearby, in one of those suburbs with walls behind which the rich live so safely, at a mall there. Tempted by a Lexus, he settled on a Honda Accord. That's what this country does, of course, it holds out temptation after temptation, forever building appetites that can't be assuaged. He didn't know if the Crown Vic was on anyone's list yet, but over the past few days he'd pushed it pretty hard. Probably time to change mounts. He left it there by the Accord. The whole exchange took perhaps five minutes.

For that matter, he had no reason to believe anyone might be on him, but one didn't take chances. Never move in straight lines.

He drove out of town, out into the desert, everything earth-colored so that it was difficult to say where city ended, desert began. But after a time, the walls, walls around individual houses, walls around whole communities, petered away. Lemon trees were in bloom, filling the air with their sweet sting. Bursts of vivid oleander at roadside. Imperial cactus.

The Accord handled wonderfully, a pleasure to drive. He settled back and, looking about, started to come to some sense of the life its owner lived. A small life, circumscribed, routine. Scattering bits of rainbow, a crystal keychain swung from the rear view mirror. The compartment behind the gear shift held tapes of Willie Nelson, Johnny Mathis, Enya, Van Morrison. A much-thumbed copy of *Atlas Shrugged* on the floor. The owner had tossed empty water bottles behind his seat after screwing the tops back on, so that many of them had collapsed into themselves. There were a couple of bronchodilator inhalers in the glove compartment. Find yourself without one, tap the guy next to you and borrow his: everyone in the state carries them. Physicians used to send what were then called chest patients here for their health. They came, bringing their plants and their cars with them. Drive into Phoenix, the first thing you see's a brown film on the horizon. The city diverts water from all over to keep lawns and golf courses green, buys electric power at a premium to run the city's myriad air conditioners. Its children gulp for air.

On the rear floor there were two-hundred-dollar running shoes, in the backseat itself a sweatshirt and windbreaker from Land's End, a red baseball cap, a deflated soccer ball, a thick yellow towel. In the bin just fore of the gearshift he found the notice of a bank overdrawal that George Hassler (he knew the name from the registration) had crumpled and thrown there. Angrily?

America.

Was there any more alien a landscape than the one in which he found himself—this long, trailing exhaust of desert, mountains forever in the distance—anywhere? He drove across dry runnels marked Coyote Wash or Aqua Fria River, chugged in the new carapace past piles, pillars and π's of stone to challenge Stonehenge or Carnac, past crass billboards, cement oases of gas stations, fast-food stalls and convenience stores chock full of sugary drinks, salty snacks, racks of sunglasses, souvenir T-shirts, Indian jewelry. Past those regal cactus.

They stood like sentinels, in an endless variety of configurations, on hillside and plain, some of them over 40 feet. Most never made it through their first year of life. Those that did, grew slowly. A saguaro could take 150 years to reach full height; in another 50 years it died. Some would never develop arms, while others might have two or four or six all upraised like candelabras, or dozens of them twisted and pointing in all directions. No one knew why this happened. Shallow and close to the surface, root systems ran out as much as a hundred feet, allowing the plants rapidly to soak up even minimal rainfalls. As the cactus took on water, its accordionlike pleats expanded. Woodpeckers and other birds often made their way into it to nest. Some, particularly hawks and the cactus wren, preferred to nest at junctures of arm and trunk. Red-tailed hawks would build large platform nests there; they'd come back again and again, every year, till the pair stopped nesting altogether. Over a six-week period in May and June, brilliant flowers emerged atop mature cacti. These would bloom for 24 hours only, opening at night, closing forever against the heat of day.

Lizards were everywhere, and just as ancient. They scampered out from beneath tangles of cholla, crouched soaking up sun atop stones, skittered across the highway, minds clenched on memories of endless rain forests, green shade, green sunlight. Brains the size of bb shot enfolded dioramas, whole maps in stark detail, of worlds long gone, worlds long ago lost.

At a truck stop near Benson, Arizona, where the pie was excellent, a young man came up to say he'd seen him arrive in the Honda Accord. On one wall dinner plates with figures of wildlife hung among framed photographs of motorbikes and vintage automobiles; on the other, portraits of John Wayne, Elvis, Marilyn and James Dean. Out back, a crude hand-painted sign with the cameo of a Confederate soldier and the legend Rebel Cafe leaned against a creche of discarded water heaters, stoves, sinks and minor appliances from which a rheumy-eyed dog peered out, as from an undersea grotto.

The young man wore an XXL purple-and-blue plaid shirt over a red T-shirt gone dull maroon, and well-used black jeans a couple of inches too long. The back half or so of the leg bottoms had been trod to shreds. Quentin's first thought as the young man approached was that he wore a baseball cap in the currently fashionable front-to-back style. But now he saw it was a skullcap. Knit, like those he'd seen on Africans.

"Had the Accord long?"

Quentin looked up at the young man. For all the alarm his question set off, this was obviously no cop. No more challenge or anxiety in those eyes than in Quentin's own. He approved, too, of the way the young man held back, staying on his feet, not presuming. Quentin nodded to the young man to join him. A corner booth. Nondescript beige plastic covering, blue paint above. Carpentry tacks stood out like a line of small brass turtles crossing the horizon.

"Had one myself," the young man said. "Accord, just like yours. Got off from work one day, came out and it was gone. First time I ever talked to police face to face."

The waitress came to refill Quentin's coffee. He asked if the young man wanted anything. He shook his head.

"Same week, my apartment got broken into. Took the stereo, TV, small appliances, most of the clothes. Even hauled off a footlocker I'd had since college, filled with God knows what. I came home from a six-mile run, took one look around, and said fuck it. Knew at some level I'd been *wanting* this to happen. Clear the decks. Free me to start over."

Sipping his third cup of coffee, Quentin watched truckers as they bowed heads over eggs and ham, looking to be in prayer. From nearby booths drifted strains of pragmatic seductions, complaints about jobs and wives, political discussions. A hash of all the age-old songs.

In the car the young man fell asleep almost at once. He'd propped feet on his duffel bag; the world bucked up unseen, unfired upon, in the notch of his knees. Choppy piano music played on the local university station. Quentin hit Scan. Sound and world alike tilted all about him, falling away, rearranging itself. Rock, country, news, chatter. Stone, cactus, wildflowers, trailer park.

Awake now, Quentin's passenger said, "Where are we?"

"Pretty much where we were before. It's only been a couple of hours."

He thought about that.

"Damn."

Roadside, an elderly Latino sold cabbage, cucumbers and bags of peppers out of the bed of his truck, the cover of which unfolded and sat atop rough wood legs to form a tent. A younger woman (daughter? wife?) sat on the ground in the shade of the truck, reading.

"Where we going?" Quentin's passenger said.

"East."

Towards El Paso, one of America's great in-between cities. They ate in a truck stop on I-10 just outside Los Cruces, a place the size of a gymnasium smelling of onions, hot grease and deisel. Meat loaf was the daily special, with mashed potatoes and boiled cabbage on the side. Using his fork like a squeegee, Quentin's passenger scraped his plate clean, then caught up with a piece of bread what miniscule leavings remained.

Eschewing the interstate, Quentin took the long way in, the back road as locals say, Route 28, skirting fields of cotton, chilis, onions and alfalfa, tunneling through the 2.7-mile green, cool canopy of Stahman

Farm's pecan orchards, up past San Miguel, La Mesa, Chambertino, La Union. The sun was settling into the cleft of the mountains to the left, throwing out its net of evening to reel the world in. As they pulled onto Mesa, parking lots outside shops and offices were emptying, streets filling with cars, street lights coming on.

"You can let me out up at that corner," Quentin's passenger said. "Appreciate the ride. Looks like a good place, El Paso. For a while." He leaned back into the window. "They're all good places for a while, right?"

Dinner became caldo and chicken mole at Casa Herado, the rest of the evening a movie on the cable channel at La Quinta off Mesa on Remcon Circle.

In the space between seat and door on passenger's side, Quentin found a well-worn wallet bound with rubber bands and containing a driver's license, social security card and two or three low-end charge cards for James Parker. Left behind, obviously, by his passenger. Had the young man stolen it, lifted it, liberated it? Much of the gypsy about him, no doubt about that. But mostly Quentin remembered the young man's remarks about becoming free, starting over.

By five in the morning, light in hot pursuit, Quentin was on Transmountain Road heading through Smuggler's Pass to Rim Road where, at one of the slumbering residential palaces there, he swapped the Honda for a Crown Vic. Some banker or real estate salesman would greet the morning with unaccustomed surprise. Quentin hoped the man liked his new car. His own smelt faintly of cigars, spilled milk and bourbon. Wires had hung below the dash even before those Quentin tugged out and touched together. But when he goosed the accelerator in query, the car shuddered and roared to let him know it was ready.

YEARS AGO IN Texas, Quentin had witnessed an execution. The whole lethal injection thing was new back then, and no one knew just how to proceed. Some sort of ritual seemed in order, though, so things were said by the warden, a grizzled, stoop-shouldered man looking twice his probable age, then by a tow-headed chaplain looking half his. It was difficult to find much to say. Casey Cortland had led a wholly unremarkable, all but invisible life before one warm Friday evening in the space of an hour killing his wife of twelve years, his ten-year-old son and eight-year-old daughter, and the lay minister of a local church. Cortland was brought in and strapped to a table. Beneath prison overalls, Quentin knew, he was diapered. Unlike the warden and chaplain, Cortland had no final words. When they injected the fatal drug, he seized: the IV line pulled out and went flying, dousing all those seated close by with toxic chemicals. State police took Quentin, who'd caught the spray directly in his eyes, to Parkland. Though basically unharmed, for several weeks he suffered blurred vision and headaches. Hours later on the prison parking lot Quentin reclaimed his Volvo, then I-30. Hour by hour, chunks of Texas broke off and fell away in his rear view mirror. That night he had the dream for the first time. In the dream, along with an estimated half-million other viewers he watched as Tiffany's father was eaten on camera, the mid-morning show live, producers and cameramen too stunned to shut it all down. Tiffany used to have a pair of earrings with the bottom half of a man hanging out of a shark's mouth. That's not what it was like. It wasn't like anything Quentin or other viewers had ever seen. Tiffany's father's legs rolled back and forth, feet pointing north-northeast, north-northwest, as the tiger chewed and pawed and pulled back its head to tear away chunks. There were sounds. Screams at first, then not so many. Gristle sounds, bone sounds. Growls. Or was it purring? Panels of experts, rapidly assembled, offered explanations of what this event said about society's implicit violence. Then Tiffany herself was there, sobbing into the microphone held close to her face like a second, bulbous nose. Daddy only did it for her, she said. He did everything for her.

ALL THAT DAY off and on, Back Then as he now thought of it, Quentin had spent writing a letter he hoped might persuade Allied's insurance carriers to reconsider Sandy Buford's claim. Every two minutes the phone rang, people kept washing up from the passageway outside his cubicle, his boss broke in like a barge with queries re one or another file, the list of calls to return and calls to be made seemed as always to grow longer instead of shorter. Sandy had hurt his back on the job and now, following surgery, wasn't able to lift the poundage Allied's job description required. He was a good worker, with the company over fourteen years. But since the surgeon had released him and he couldn't meet the job's bottom line—even though Sandy's actual work from day to day didn't call for lifting—the insurance carrier had begun disallowing all claims, refusing payment to physicians, labs and physical therapists, and effectively blocking the company's efforts to reemploy him. Quentin's letter summarized the case in concise detail, explained why Allied believed the carrier's disallowment to be inappropriate and in error, and put forth a convincing argument (Quentin hoped) for reevaluation.

Pulling out of the parking lot at 6:18, just a little over an hour late leaving, on the spur of the moment Quentin decided to swing by Sandy Buford's and drop off a copy of the letter, let him know someone cared. Quentin had called to let Ellie know how late he was running; she was expecting him home. But this would only take a few minutes.

Buford's address bore him to a sea of duplexes and shabby apartment buildings at city's edge. Many of them looked like something giant children, given blocks and stucco, might erect. Discarded appliances formed victory gardens in side and back yards. Long-dead cars and trucks sat in driveways, ancient life forms partially reconstructed from remains.

Quentin waded through front yards that may well have seen conga lines of children dancing their parents' preference for Adlai Stevenson over Ike (when had people stopped caring that much?) and climbed a stairwell where the Rosenbergs' execution could have been a major topic of discussion. One expected the smell of cooking cabbage. These days the smell of Quarter Pounders, Whoppers, Pizza Hut and KFC were far more likely, maybe a bit of cumin or curry mixed in.

Buford's apartment was on the third floor. There was music playing inside, sounded like maybe a TV as well, but no one responded to Quentin's knocks. Finally he pushed a copy of the letter, tucked into an Allied Beverage pay envelope, beneath it. He was almost to the second landing when he heard four loud cracks, like limbs breaking. Instinctively he drew back against the wall as two young men burst from the apartment nearest the stairwell. Both wore nylon stockings over their faces. Quentin moved forward, peered over the bannister just as one of them after pulling off his stocking glanced up.

That was the footprint he left.

Careful to give the two men ample time to exit, Quentin continued down the stairs. He was turning the corner onto Central in his Taurus when the first police cars came barreling down it.

A dozen blocks along, he began to wonder if those were the same headlights behind him. He turned onto Magnolia, abruptly into the parking lot at Cambridge Arms, pulled back out onto Elm. Still there. Same brilliance, same level, dipping a beat or so after he dipped, buoying up moments later. He pulled into a Sonic and ordered a drink. Drove on a half mile or more before pulling up at the curb and getting out, motor left idling, to buy the early edition of tomorrow's newspaper. No lights behind him when he took to the street. Whoever it had been, back there, following him, was gone. If there'd been anyone. Only his imagination, most likely.

He said nothing of this to Ellie, neither as they had a preprandial glass of wine before the fireplace, nor as she pulled plates of flank steak, mashed potatoes and brussels sprouts, foil covered, from the oven, nor as, afterwards, they sat before the lowering fire with coffee. He spoke, instead, of the minutiae of his day. Office politics, the latest barge of rumor and gossip making its way upriver, cylinders banging, his concern over Sandy Buford. She shared in turn the minutiae of *her* day, including a visit to Dr. Worrell.

Head against his shoulder, 12:37 when last he glanced at the clock bedside, Ellie fell fast asleep. Quentin himself was almost asleep when he heard the crash of a window downstairs.

THE CAR HESITATES, only a moment, though it must seem forever, there at the lip.

He's not sure of any of this, of course. Not sure if it really happened, how it happened, where or when. More than once he's thought it might be only something suggested to him by a therapist; something he's read or seen on the dayroom TV whose eye is as bleary and unfocused as those of its watchers; something that he's imagined, a dream breaking like a whale from the depths of that long sleep. Yet it keeps coming back—like that other dream of a man being eaten by a tiger on live TV. Again and again in his mind's eye he *sees* it. It's as real as the plastic furniture, coffee makers and floor polishers around him—realer than most things in this world he's begun reentering. But mind is only a screen, upon which anything may be projected.

Go on, then.

The car hesitates there at the lip.

With no warning a woman's nude body, pale as the moon, had stepped into his headlights on that barren stretch of road. Flying saucers might just as well have set down beside him.

He'd left Cave Creek half an hour past. No houses or much of anything else out here, no lights, headlights or other cars, this time of night at least, few signs of human life at all, just this vast scoop of dark sky above and, at the edge of his lights, vague huddled shapes of low scrub, creosote, cholla, prickly pear. Further off the road, tall saguaro with arms upraised—then the heavier darkness of sawtooth mountains.

Had he a destination in mind? Into Phoenix via some roundabout route to take dinner at a crowded restaurant perhaps, hopscotching over his isolation, his loneliness? Or, as he pushed ever deeper into the desert, did he mean to flee something else altogether, the dribble of headlights on gravel roads about him, high-riding headlights of trucks and SUVs behind, silhouettes of houses on hills half a mile away, himself?

His name was Parker.

He'd taken over a light-struck house with exposed beams and white shutters, leaving behind, at the apartment where he'd been staying, the pump of accordions through open windows, songs whose tag line always seemed to be *mi corazon*, afternoons filled with the sound of stationary racing motors from tanklike ancient Fords and Buicks being worked on in the parking lot. Coyotes at twilight walked three or four to the pack down the middle of streets. First night there, he'd sat watching a hawk fall from the sky to carry off a cat. The cat had come over to investigate this new person or say hello. It had leapt onto the halfwall facing his front door, ground to wall in that effortless, levitating way they have, here one moment, there the next. Then just as suddenly the hawk had appeared—swooping away with the cat into a sunset like silent bursting shells.

He remembered eating dinner, some pasta concoction he had only to pop into the microwave. Then he'd gone outside with a bottle of wine, watching day bleed away to its end, watching the hawk make off with the cat, watching as night parachuted grandly into the mountains. He'd gone in to watch part of a movie, then, bottle depleted, decided on a ride. In the car he found a tape of Indian flute music. Drove off, empty himself, into the desert's greater and somehow comforting emptiness.

Till the nude woman appeared before him.

Again: he has no idea how much of this is actual; how much remembered, suggested, imagined. Why, just returned from a turnabout trip to New York, and at that time of night, would he have driven off into the desert—driven anywhere, for that matter? What could have borne him off the highway onto that road, through fence breaks and boulders, up the bare mountainside, to its edge? What could the woman have been doing there, nude, in his headlights?

Seeing her, he swerves, instinctively left, away from the rim, but fetches up against a rise there and slides back, loose stone giving way at his rear when he hits his brakes.

The car rocks back.

In the moment before his windshield fills with dark sky and stars, he sees her there before the car, arms out like a bullfighter, breasts swaying. Braid of dark hair. In his rear view mirror, a canyon of the sort Cochise and his men might have used, subterranean rivers from which they'd suddenly rise into the white man's world to strike, into which they'd sink again without trace.

Though the car's motor has stalled, the tape plays on as the flutist begins to sing wordlessly behind the breath of his instrument, providing his own ghostly accompaniment. A lizard scampers across the windshield. Music, sky and lizard alike go with him over the edge and down—down for a long time.

His name, the name of the person to whom this happens, is Parker.

WITHOUT THOUGHT, HE left her there.

Acting purely on instinct, he was halfway across the roof before anything like actual thought or volition came, before the webwork of choices began forming in his mind. Never let the opponent choose the ground. Withdraw, lure the opponent onto your own, or at least onto neutral ground. By then years of training and action had broken over him like a flood. Four days later, on a Monday, Quentin stood looking down at two bodies. These were the men he'd seen fleeing the apartment below Sandy Buford's. For a moment it was Ellie's body he saw there on the floor of that faceless motel room. He knew from newspaper accounts that the two of them had spent some time at the house once he'd fled. He tried not to think how long, tried not to imagine what had happened there.

Surprisingly, as in the old days, he bore them no direct ill will. They were working men like himself, long riders, dogs let loose on the grounds.

Himself who, hearing the window crash downstairs, rolled from bed onto his feet and was edging out onto the roof even as footsteps sounded on the stairs. Then was up and over.

With small enough satisfaction he took their car, a mid-range Buick. A simple thing to pull wires out from beneath the dash, cross them. Somewhere in it he would find the map he needed, something about the car would guide him. He had that faith. Everyone left footprints.

Never blame the cannon. Find the hands that set elevation, loaded and primed it, lit the fuse. Find the mouth that gave the order.

They'd have to die, of course, those two. But that was only the beginning.

THE WORLD COMES back by degrees. There are shapes, patterns of dark and light, motion that corresponds in some vague way to sounds arriving from out there. They knock at your door with luggage in hand, these sounds. While in here you have a great deal of time to think, to sink back into image and sensation in which language has no place. Again and again you see a sky strewn with stars, a lizard's form huge among them, a woman's pale body.

Constantly, it seems, you are aware of your breathing as an envelope that surrounds you, contains you.

For some reason flute music, itself a kind of breath, remains, tendrils of memory drifting through random moments of consciousness. Memory and present time have fused. Each moment's from a book. You page backward, forward, back again. All of it has the same import, same imprimatur.

Faces bend close above you. When you see them, they all look the same. You're fed bitter pastes of vegetables and meat. Someone pulls at your leg, rotates the ankle, pushes up on the ball of your foot to flex it. Two women talk overhead, about home and boyfriends and errant children, as they roll you side to side, wiping away excrement, changing sheets. One day you realize that you can feel the scratchiness, the warmth, of their washclothes.

The TV is left on all the time. At night (you know it's night because no one disturbs you then) the rise and fall of this voice proves strangely comforting. Worst is midmorning when everything goes shrill: voices of announcers and game-show hosts, the edgy canned laughter of sitcoms, commercials kicked into overdrive.

There are, too, endless interrogations. At first, even when you can't, even when it's all you can do to keep from drowning in the flood of words and you're wholly unable to respond, you try to answer. Further along, having answered much the same queries for daily generations of social workers, medical students and interns, you refuse to participate, silent now for quite a different reason.

The world comes back by degrees, and slowly, by degrees, you understand that it's not the world you left. Surreptitious engineers have sneaked in and built a new world while you slept. In this world you're but a tourist, a visitor, an impostor. They'll find you out, some small mistake you'll make.

Mr. Parker, do you know where you are?

Can you tell me what happened?

Can you move your hand, feet, eyes?

Do you know who's President?

Is there anything you need?

"No."

HERE IS WHAT my visitor tells me.

We met, Julie and this Parker, just out of school, both still dragging along cumbersome ideals that all but dwarfed us. Once, she said, I told her how as a kid I'd find insects in drawers and cabinets lugging immense, stagecoach-like egg cases behind. That's what it was like.

We had our own concept of manifest destiny, Julie said. No doubt about it, it was up to us to change the world. We'd have long conversations over pizza at The Raven, beer at the Rathskeller, burgers at Maple Street Cafe: What could we do? Push a few books back into place and the world's shelves would be in order again? We fancied ourselves chiropractors of chaos and corruption: one small adjustment here, a realignment there, all would come straight.

Colonialism. Chile and the CIA. South Africa, Vietnam, our own inner cities, Appalachia. We imagined we were unearthing all manner of rare truth, whereas in truth, as immensely privileged middle-class whites, we were simply learning what most of the world had known forever.

When I found out you were here, I had to come, she says. How long has it been? Twenty years?

She works as a volunteer at the hospital. Saw my name on the admissions list and thought: Could it possibly be?

OTHER THINGS YOU begin to remember:

The smell of grapefruit from the back yard of the house across the alley from your apartment.

The rustle of pigeons high overhead in the topknots of palm trees.

Geckos living in a crack in the wall outside your window. By daylight larger lizards come out onto the ledge and rest there. Lizard aerobics: they push their bodies up onto extended legs. Lizard hydraulics: they ease back down.

Dry river beds.

Empty swimming pools painted sky blue.

Mountains.

Even in the center of the city, you're always within sight of mountains. Mornings, they're shrouded in smog, distant, surreal and somehow pre-historic, as though just now, as slowly the earth warms, taking form. Late-afternoon sunlight breaks through clouds in fanlike shafts, washes the mountains in brilliance, some of them appearing black as though burned, others in close relief. Spectacular sunsets break over them at night—and plunge into them.

Sometimes you'd drive into the desert with burritos or a bottle of wine to witness those sunsets. Other times you'd go out there to watch storms gather. Doors fell open above you: great tidal waves of wind and lightning, the whole sky alive with fire.

This is when you were alive.

"YOU'RE GOING TO be okay, Mr. Parker."

Her name, I remember, though I check myself with a glance at her nametag, is Marcia. On the margins of the nametag, which is the size of a playing card, she has pasted tiny pictures of rabbits and angels.

"The doctors will be in to speak with you shortly."

I wonder just how they'll speak with me shortly. Use abbreviations, clipped phrases or accents, some special form of semaphore taught them in medical school? One rarely understands what they say in all earnest.

Marcia is twenty-eight. Her husband left her six months ago, she now lives in a garage apartment with an ex-biker truck driver named Jesse. To this arrangement Jesse has brought a baggage of tattoos (including two blue jailhouse tears at the edge of one eye) and his impression of life as a scrolling roadway, six hundred miles to cover before his day and daily case of beer are done. To this arrangement she's brought a four-year-old daughter, regular paychecks and notions of enduring love. Hers is the heavier burden.

I've paid attention, watched closely, hoping to learn to pass here in this new world. I know the lives of these others just as, slowly, I am retrieving my own.

Of course it's my own.

Marcia leans over me, wraps the bladder of the blood-pressure monitor about my arm, inflates it.

"It's coming back to you, isn't it?"

Some of it.

"No family that you know of?"

None.

"I'm sorry. Families are a good thing at times like this."

She tucks the blood-pressure cuff behind its wall gauge and plucks the digital thermometer from beneath my tongue, ejecting its sheath into the trash can.

"Things are going to be tough for a while. Hate to think about your having to go it alone," she says, turning back at the door. "Need anything else right now?"

No.

I turn my head to the window. Hazy white sky out there, bright. Always bright in Phoenix, Valley of the Sun. Maybe when I get out I'll move to Tucson, always have liked Tucson. Its uncluttered streets and mountains and open sky, the way the city invites the desert in to live.

With a perfunctory knock at the door, Marcia reenters.

"Almost forgot." A Post-It Note. "Call when you can, she says."

Julie.

Back when we first met we'd walk, late afternoons, along Turtle Creek, downtown Dallas out of sight to one side, Highland Park to the other, as Mercedes, Beamers and the bruised, battered, piled-high trucks of Hispanic gardeners made their ways home on the street. Just up the rise, to either side of Cedar Springs, bookstores, guitar shops and tiny ethnic restaurants straggled. Within the year glassy, brickfront office buildings took up residence and began staring them down. Within the year, all were gone.

She tells me this when she comes to visit.

Twenty years.

She never had children. Her husband died eight years ago. She has a cat. I've thought of you often, Julie says.

TUCKED INTO A compartment in the driver's door Quentin found a rental agreement. When you need a car, rentals are always a good bet. You can identify them from the license plates mostly, and no one gets in a hurry over stolen rentals. The contract was with Dr. Samuel Taylor, home address Iowa City, local address c/o William Taylor at an ASU dorm. Mr. Taylor had paid by Visa. Good chance he was visiting a son, then, and that the car had been boosted somewhere in Tempe. Quentin called the rental agency, saying he'd seen some Hispanic teenagers who looked like they didn't belong in this car, noticed the plate, and was checking to see if it might have been reported stolen. But he couldn't get any information from the woman who answered the phone, and hung up when she started demanding his name and location.

A dead end.

He left his motel room (first floor rear, alley behind, paid for with cash) and went back to the Buick. He wasn't driving it, but he'd left it out of sight where he could get to it.

Neither of them had smoked. Radio buttons were set at three oldie stations, one country, one easy listening. The coat folded on the backseat he assumed to be Dr. Taylor's; few enforcers (if that's what the two were) wore camel's hair. Likewise the leather attaché case tucked beneath the driver's seat, which, at any rate, held nothing of interest. The paperback under the passenger's seat was a different matter. *Lesbian Wife*, half the pages so poorly impressed as to be all but unreadable. Tucked in between page 34 and 35 was a cash ticket from Good Night Motel.

Good Night Motel proved a miracle of cheap construction and tacky cover-up the builder no doubt charged off as architectural highlights. The clerk inside was of similar strain, much preoccupied with images on a six-inch TV screen alongside an old-style brass cash register. However he tried to direct them away, his eyes kept falling back to it.

"Look, I'm just here days," he said, scant moments after Quentin tired of equivocations and had braced to drag him bodily across the desk's chipped formica. "Never saw them. Might check at the bar." And heaved a sigh as a particularly gripping episode of *Gilligan's Island* was left unspoiled?

In contrast to the inertial desk clerk, the barkeep was a wiry little guy who couldn't be still. He twitched, twisted, moved salt shakers, coasters and ashtrays around as though playing himself in a board game, drummed fingers on the bar top. He had a thin moustache and sharp features. Something of the rat about him.

Quentin asked for brandy, got a blank stare and changed his request to a draft with whiskey back. He put a fifty on the bar.

"I don't have change."

"You won't need it."

Quentin described the two men. The barkeep nudged a bin of lime wedges square into its cradle.

"Sure, they been in. Three, four nights this week. Not last night, though. One does shots, Jack Daniels. Other's a beer man. Friends of yours?"

"Purely professional. Guys have money coming, from an inheritance. Lawyers hired me to find them."

"Sure they did."

Quentin pushed the fifty closer.

"That covers the drinks. People I work for—"

"Lawyers, you mean."

"Right. The lawyers. Been known to be big tippers."

Another fifty went on the counter, closer to Quentin than to the bartender.

"Four blocks down, south corner, Paradise Motor Hotel. Saw them turn in there on my way home one night. Bottom line kind of place, the Paradise. No bar, no place to eat. Gotta hoof it to Denny's a dozen blocks uptown. Or come here."

Quentin pushed the second fifty onto the first.

"Freshen that up for you?" the barkeep asked.

"Why not?"

He waved away Quentin's offer of payment. "This one's on me."

Afterwards—it all happened quickly and more or less silently, no reason to think he'd be interrupted—Quentin searched that faceless motel room. Nothing. Sport coats and shirts hanging in the closet, usual toiletries by the bathroom sink, a towel showing signs of dark hair dye. Couple issues of *Big Butt* magazine.

Quentin went downstairs and across rippled asphalt to the office, set into a bottleneck of an entryway that let whoever manned the desk watch all comings and goings. Today a woman in her mid-twenties manned it. She looked the way librarians do in movies from the Fifties. This kind of place, a phone deposit was required if you planned to use it, and even local calls had to go through the desk. They got charged to the room. The records, of course, are private. Of course they are, he responded – and should be. Twenty dollars further on, they became less private. Another dour Lincoln and Quentin was looking at them. He wondered what she might do with the money. Nice new lanyard for her glasses, special food for the cat?

There'd been one call to 528-1000 (Pizza Palace), two to 528-1888 (Ming's Chinese), and three to 528-1433. That last was a lawyer's office in a strip mall clinging like a barnacle to city's edge, flanked by a cut-rate shoe store and family clothing outlet. Like many of his guild, David Cohen proved reluctant to answer questions in a direct, forthright manner. Quentin soon convinced him.

Bradley C. Smith was quite a different animal, his lair no motel room or strip-mall office but a house in the city's most exclusive neighborhood, built (as though to make the expense of it all still more evident) into a hillside. Location was everything. That's what real-estate agent Bradley C. Smith told his clients. But real estate was only one of Bradley C. Smith's vocations. His influence went far and wide; he was a man with real power.

But that power for many years now had insulated Bradley C. Smith from confrontation. That power depended on money, middle men, lawyers, enforcers, collectors, accountants. None of which were present when Quentin stepped into the powerful man's bathroom just as Bradley C. Smith emerged naked, flesh pale as a mushroom, from the shower.

There at the end, Bradley C. Smith tried to tell him more. Seemed desperate to tell him, in fact. That was what, at the end, Bradley C. Smith seized upon, holding up a trembling hand again and again, imploring with eyes behind which light was steadily fading.

Thing was, Quentin didn't care. Now he knew why the two killers had been dispatched to that apartment on Sycamore, now he had the other name he needed. Ultimately, those two had little to do with him, with his life, with the door he was pushing closed now. Soon they'd have nothing at all to do with it, neither those two, nor Bradley C. Smith, nor the other. Quentin walked slowly down the stairs, climbed into his stolen Volvo. Soon enough it would be over, all of it.

I FAIL TO recognize myself in mirrors, or in Julie's memories, or in many of my own.

I remember riding in a car with a young man dressed strangely, in a plaid shirt that hung on him like a serape, black bell bottoms, an African skullcap. Remember finding a wallet bound with rubber bands once he'd gone.

I remember lying prone in a church steeple watching families come and go.

I remember a man drifting away from me in a culvert, blue dye coloring the water beneath him. Bodies below me on a motel room floor. Other bodies, many of them, half a world away.

As memory returns, it does so complexly – stereophonically. There is what I am told of Parker, a set of recollections and memories that seem to belong to him, and, alongside those, these other memories of bodies and cars, green jungles, deserts, a kind of double vision in which everything remains forever just out of focus, blurred.

I wonder if this might not be how the mind functions in madness: facts sewn loosely together, so that contrasting, contradictory realities are held in suspension, simultaneously, in the mind, scaffolds clinging to the faceless, sketchy edifice of actuality.

"I BROUGHT YOU some coffee. Real coffee. Figured you could use it. I've had my share of what hospitals call coffee."

He set the cup, from Starbuck's, on the bedside table.

"Thank you."

"Don't mention it. City paid. You need help with that top?"

Parker swung his legs over bed's edge and sat, pried off the cover. The detective remained standing, despite the chair close by.

Light gray suit, something slightly off about the seams. Plucked from a mark-down rack at Mervyn's, Dillard's? Blue shirt that had ridden with him through many days just like this one, darkish red tie that from the look of deformations above and below the knot must turn out a different length most times it got tied. Clothes don't make the man, but they rarely fail to announce to the world who he thinks he might be.

"Sergeant Wootten. Bill." He sipped from his own cup. "You don't have kids, do you, Mr. Parker?"

Parker shook his head. The sergeant shook his in turn.

"My boy? Sixteen? I swear I don't know what to make of him, haven't for years now. Not long ago he was running with a crowd they all had tattoos, you know? Things like beercan tabs in their ears, little silver balls hanging out of their noses. Then a month or so back he comes down to breakfast in a dark blue suit, been wearing it ever since. Go figure."

"What can I do for you, Sergeant?"

"Courtesy visit, more or less."

"You realize that I remember almost nothing of what happened?"

"Yes, sir. I'm aware of that. Very little of what happened, and nothing from before. But paperwork's right up there with death, taxes and tapeworms. Can't get away from it."

Holding up the empty cup, Parker told him thanks for the coffee. The sergeant took Parker's cup, slipped his own inside it, dropped both in the trash can by the door.

"I've read your statement, the accident reports, spoke with your doctors. No reason in any of that to take this any further."

He walked to the window and stood quietly a moment.

"Beautiful day. Not that most of them aren't." He turned back. "Still don't have a handle on what happened out there."

"Nor do I. You know what I remember of it. The rest is gone."

"Could come back to you later on, the doctors say. They also say you're out of here tomorrow. Going home."

"Out of here, anyway."

"We'll need a contact address in case something else comes up. Not that anything's likely to. Give us a call."

The sergeant held out his hand. Quentin shook it.

"Best of luck to you, Mr. Parker."

When he was almost to the door: "One thing still bothers me, though. We can't seem to find any record of you for these past four years. Where you were living, what you were doing. Almost like you didn't exist."

"I've been in Europe."

"Well that's it then, isn't it. Like I said: best of luck, Mr. Parker."

THERE WAS A time alone then, first in an apartment off Van Buren in central Phoenix where Quentin found comfort in the slam of car doors and the banging of wrenches against motors, in the rich roll of calls in Spanish across the parking lot and between buildings, in the pump and chug of accordions and conjunto bands from radios left on, it seemed, constantly; then, thinking he wanted to be truly alone, in an empty house just outside Cave Creek. Scouting it, he discovered credit-card receipts for two round-trip tickets to Italy, return date a month away. No neighbors within sight. He had little, few possessions, to move in. He parked the car safely away from the house.

There was a time, too, of aimless, intense driving, to Flagstaff, Dallas,

El Paso, even once all the way to New York, road trips in which he'd leave the car only to eat and sleep, as often as not selecting some destination at random and driving there only to turn around and start back.

He thought little about his life before, about the four men he had killed, still less about his present life. It was as though he were suspended, waiting for something he could feel moving towards him, something that had been moving towards him for a long time.

"THANKS FOR PICKING me up."

"You're welcome. Guess I'd been kind of hoping you'd call."

They pulled onto Black Canyon Freeway. Late afternoon, and traffic was heavy, getting heavier all the time, lines of cars zooming out of the cattle chutes. Clusters of industrial sheds—automotive specialty shops and the like—at roadside as they cleared the cloverleaf, then bordering walls above which thrust the narrow necks of palm trees and signage, sky beyond. The world was so full. Ribbons of scarlet, pink and chrome yellow blew out on the horizon as the sun began settling behind sawtooth mountains. Classical music on low, the age-old, timeless ache of cellos.

The world was so full.

"Had breakfast?" Julie asked.

Caught unawares, she'd thrown an old sweatshirt over grass-stained white jeans a couple sizes too large. Cheeks flushed, hair still wet from the shower. Nonetheless she'd taken time to ferret out and bring him a change of clothes. Her husband's, Parker assumed. They had the smell of long storage about them.

"Little late for that, don't you think?"

"Breakfast's a state of mind. Like so much of life. More about rebirth, things starting up again, knowing they can, than it is about time of day. It's also my favorite meal."

"Never was much of a breakfast person myself."

"You should give it a try."

"You're right. I should."

She nodded. "There's a great café just ahead, breakfast twenty-fours a day, best in the valley. You got time?"

"I don't have much else."

"Good. We'll stop, then. After that . . . You have a place to stay?"

"No."

"Yes," Julie said. "Yes. You do."

New Life

OVER PAST DAYS a speed bump has grown in the street just outside my living room. Each day, morning and again late afternoon, crews pull up in their trucks to nurture the speed bump, to feed it, water it, bring it forth. Out of the open backs of their trucks they unload cannisters, hand tools and blowtorches, pots of white paint, small appliances like lawn edgers, saws, a huge curved bar, buckets, baskets. Behind my window, behind the veil of its covering, day by day I watch the speed bump take form. At first it's but a stretch of new asphalt, shining and black beneath the noonday sun. Later that day the crews come and, with one member directing flame towards it, another wielding a kind of long hoe, shape it into a perfect rectangle. Gradually over following days an actual hump develops. The speed bump begins to look like the back of some largely submerged creature. That night I stand for a long time watching it in moonlight. The next morning, when they paint white stripes across it, I realize how beautiful it is becoming.

"Are you going to finish your breakfast?" Alice asks.

I look back at the melon, fresh-sliced bread and tub of butter, the thick bacon she drives all the way across town, to AJ's, to buy, none of which looks appetizing any longer. I shake my head, say I'm really not hungry.

"They're at it awfully early."

Of course. This is important work. The city's not inert. Like a forest, it's alive, ever growing, ever changing. And these, these workmen dismounting twice daily from their trucks, are the city's vaqueros, its shepherds, its midwives.

"If you want me to drop you, you'd better get dressed."

So I put on my dark blue suit, light blue shirt with tiny buttons at the collar, lemon tie, and pull on oxblood leather loafers. I'm almost ready when I hear the kitchen door, and have to go scampering out to catch up with Alice. She stands watching as driver after driver speeds down the street and hits the bump. Two or three of them bottom out on reentry; one, bouncing frantically, swerves onto the sidewalk. Alice smiles.

At the office I sit looking out over the ramparts, spires and depressions that form the city. These in the window echo the graphs before me on my computer screen. We're fifteen floors up, sharing altitude only with traffic helicopters, window cleaners hauled up by their platform's bootstraps, and hawks who thrive on the city's pigeons. All along the vena cava of interstate, carotids of the roundabout near city hall, arteries, arterioles, capillaries, traffic moves unimpeded.

"Ralph?"

Vicky says it again. For the second time? third?

"You want something from Armando's? We're ordering out."

No, I tell her, vague recollections of cups of black coffee in my mind. How many cups have I had? When had I last eaten? A single piece of bread this morning, a bite of melon. Last night I'd twirled my fork in the bowl of angel hair (olive oil, garlic, black olives and Parmesan) before pushing it away. At bowl's bottom, like some cartoon character on a child's, was a scene from Provence. But I was not to go there.

Vicky, meanwhile, has paused thoughtfully at the entrance to my cubicle. "You really need to start taking care of yourself. You can't work all the time."

"I don't."

"Little wheels and lights, Ralph."

"What?"

"They're there all the time, behind your eyes."

"Nonsense."

"Okay." She turns and is gone, only to be replaced by Miss Allen. Everyone is waiting for me in the conference room, Miss Allen says.

In the presence of senior partners and clients, sipping further cups of coffee in an effort to energize self and delivery (not much I can do about lack of substance), I stumble through my half-prepared presentation.

"Thank you, Ralph," Mr. Townsend says afterwards. A Roman candle launched into silence.

"It went. Definitely it went," I say that night when Alice asks me over pork and yucca spooned from the crock pot and served over rice how my day had gone. "Yours?"

"I think we found a foster home for Jimmie Vaste, a good one."

Jimmie is a twelve-year-old of ambiguous and indeed ambivalent sexuality, one of those kids who by turns disturbs, charms, offends and terrifies adults. Looking into his eyes is like peering into a tank of water where, just out of sight, something sinister turns and glides. Alice must see placing him as a grand coup.

"Congratulations," I tell her, pushing pork, yucca and rice around on my plate, amazed as always that in her work she deals with people, with actual human situations. Quite different from my own. Paradigm makes nothing, produces nothing, adds nothing to the world. We're Movers-Around, taking things from one place and putting them elsewhere: paperwork, resources, companies, executives, armies of workers, products. No one can touch Paradigm at Moving Around.

Climbing up from the dinner table, Alice and I pour single malt Scotch from the Orkney Islands into crystal glasses and carry it, as though it's not already travelled far enough, with coffee, out to the living room. I'll come back and clean up, clear the table, wash dishes, later. We settle in among framed posters of art exhibits and dance recitals, reproductions of Ingres and Thomas Cole, blond bent-wood furniture. Alice lifts her current read, a history of Egypt, from the table alongside, opens to the bookmark and all but visibly sinks in. I read a page or so of a novel titled *Pale Mountain* and, realizing I've no idea what I just read, go back to the beginning. The journey's no better this time around, or the next. From the CD system Robert Johnson declaims *I'm booked and I got to go.*

Where *I* go is to the window.

The black back of the beast gleams brighter than ever in moonlight, its white stripes have gone luminous. Because of these stripes the far side of the speed bump appears convex, the nearer concave. A late-model Buick turns in off Seventh Street and pulls up, sits for a moment before the speed bump, headlights a bright carpet. Then it moves slowly backwards, swings into a driveway, and pulls out heading back the way it came. Its headlights lash across our wall.

"Are you coming to bed?" Alice asks behind me.

Oh yes, I say. And fall into the swathe of moonlight there beside her, my love, my life.

Surely it's only my imagination, these sounds I hear outside, as of something taking its first uncertain steps and beginning to move steadily along the street.

Roofs and Forgiveness in the Early Dawn

THEY STARTED EARLY tonight. Susan and I sat listening to their legs dragging across the roof and shutters, the soft snicker of their calls, the occasional brief whirr of wings. At their size, the wings aren't of much use —best they do is provide a kind of controlled fall.

Susan got up, went to the window to peer out between slats of the shutter, at the roof directly across from ours. Broken bottles baked into tar, part of what appeared to be a toaster with power cord trailing out like a tail behind, a few sacks and plastic bags of trash. One of them was dead over there, on its back. No, not dead, dying. Its legs twitched as I watched. Two others were eating it.

"They're really rather beautiful, you know. In their way."

I shrugged. Susan sees things the rest of us don't, or sees them in ways we can't. This is what makes her what she is. Against the wall opposite the window is her latest painting. Struck by morning light, half in sun, half in twilight, a sort of hive looking (inasmuch as it resembles anything at all familiar) like the communities of Anasazi cliff dwellers. Above the hive one of them hangs in midair. "They can't fly like that, of course," Susan said when I first saw it.

There can't be much food left for them here, after all these years. While we go on living off the bounty of our ancestors, cans of Spam, peas, Spaghetti-O's, tomato soup, Pepsi, corned beef hash, asparagus, sardines, potted meat, green beans.

She turned back to me. Must be a full moon out there. Light fell in a soft lash across her breasts. Her soft breasts. But they're not, really. Small and hard, rather. Dried-up, used-up, like the rest of our world.

Always desirable, though. Each night she stands at the window like this for hours before we go to bed. Yet another thing I try not to think about. What it means, how so much is different. How it all has changed.

Soon Susan was asleep. I turned on the radio, spun back and forth across the dial till I found something. You never knew. A few stations were still around and broadcast when they could. Some nights even the static was comforting.

Good morning, all you. Dark here, don't we know—but always morning somewhere. You're listening to The Voice of the People, Free Radio 102 point 4. What you've just heard was Shen O-Wah reading from her new book, Slide It In.

My God, I thought, someone is still publishing books. Susan drifted towards the surface in her sleep. She turned and moved closer to me, said (roughly) *Mmgh.* I was on my right side. Her arm came across my chest, hand hanging into space. I took it in my own and drew it to me. We were one.

Reports are just in from our watchers. Heaviest activity tonight is in the southwest part of the city,

Our part.

from riverside up to the old Beltway. That's the current hot zone. Stay tuned for updates. We'll be with you all night here. Who can sleep, after all?

Susan could, for one. There was some kind of switch in her head. She threw it and the cogs disengaged, she slowed and stopped. By contrast I felt I never slept at all and spent the night with my mind whirring about snatches of songs and thought, never quite getting purchase. I did sleep, though, I must have, because from time to time I'd rouse with tatters of dreams drifting up, there for a second or two, almost graspable, before they trailed off and were gone.

Lot of us around the station have been listening to Ornette Coleman these past weeks. Here's one of the tunes where Coleman and his crew broke through for the first time. To us, this sounds like the world we live in.

He was right, it did. So would Ravel's *La Valse.* The difference was that in *La Valse* we started out on solid ground, witnessed the unwinding, the unraveling into chaos. With Coleman, chaos was already there, waiting like slippers and robe, a comfortable pair of jeans.

I heard the whirr of wings, moments later the thump of one of them hitting the shutters outside. The six-inch spurs of its legs ground against wood, a sound like a wire brush, as it groped for footholds.

Susan, I realized, was awake.

"You remember when we thought they might just go away? We'd get up one day and they'd be gone, gone as suddenly as they appeared."

I did. We're a hopeful species. And things went well for us for a long time. Longer than we had any right to expect.

Sorry to break in. Ornette does grab on and hold, doesn't he? But new information's just come in. Our watchers tell us that activity seems to be shifting heavily towards the northeast. We don't know why. But we never do, do we?

Susan got up, went to the window. She put her hand on the glass, opposite one of its feet. At length then, she turned back to me. Light fell in a slant across her thighs.

"Do you remember birds, Jean-Luc?"

I nodded.

"I can—just barely." And such sadness in her eyes. "It's their world now."

What could I say? What could Ornette say, other than to honk away on his plastic horn? Then a scrambling rasp as our latest visitor dropped off the window, trusting itself to the grace of those lamentable wings.

"It's their world and they know it," Susan said.

It was highly unlikely, of course, that they knew anything at all, but I didn't point this out. With them all was hunger and instinct. We humans have always valued our precious intelligence far more than it deserves. My brother told me that just before he went home to dive off his fourteenth-floor balcony, almost ten years ago now. Two or three years after they began showing up.

Outside, the sky had begun to lighten. Those who hadn't already moved on across the city would be heading back now to wherever it is they go.

I looked at Susan and had a vision of her throwing back the shutters, leaning into the window. I saw her legs slide across the sill, heard the soft snicker of its call, the whirr of wings, as she fell into the arms of the future. I took her, before that happened, into my own.

Under Construction

THEY STOOD TOGETHER there in the center of the room. The man rubbed thumb against fingers, feeling the grit of dust and refuse he'd bent to lift from the floor. Turning on one foot, the woman reached to brush the wall with her hands, then brought them to her face. There were smears of grayish white on the palms, from the paint.

"It's lovely," she said.

"One of a kind," the real estate agent, a Mr. Means, told them.

"But rather dear," the man said.

"You *could* look at it that way, I suppose. Have you been looking long? Seen what's out there? I'm assuming this is your first unit together." There was a gleam in his eyes. Surgically implanted, the man had heard. He had no idea if it were true. You were always hearing these things.

The woman nodded.

"And not just everyone can appreciate character like this. An exact reproduction, you know. Here," he said, "let me show you."

Taking the two short strides needed to reach the room's far side, he pulled back what appeared to be paneling on the wall but was in fact a curtain. Man and woman alike drew startled breaths.

A window!

"Fine touch, isn't it? From an artisan upstate. Best there is. They say he worked for years just to get the staining right. Glass looks like it's been up there ten, twenty years."

Down in the street, not in the street actually, but next to it, in a long, broad alley, workmen were erecting a wall. A dozen or more stood on line, passing rough-cut blocks of stone from hand to hand. The last man in line set a stone in place atop the wall. Then he moved to the rear of the line to wait his turn as the others shifted forward.

On the way here the man and woman had come across a construction crew lined up alongside streetcar tracks. The tracks went for several blocks and ended as abruptly as they'd begun. There were no indications of further construction, or of a streetcar.

"I'm also assuming," Mr. Means said, "that this would be short term."

The woman looked first at the man, then towards the floor when he said "Of course."

"Different rates, you see. Long term, now that, you ever want to consider it, sometime in the future maybe, that one has teeth. But short term, like I brought out to you on the wire, on that I can give you a sweet deal. *Good* numbers. Wouldn't even have to run them by my handler." He smiled. "Just so you know. Now you take your time, look around all you want, get the feel of the place. I'll just stand over here, out of your way."

So saying, he took up position by the outside door. If someone came in, they might hang a coat on him without thinking. If anyone else could have got in here.

He owed this to her, owed it to himself, the man was thinking. If life couldn't have some specialness to it, something at the center that really mattered, how could it matter at all? He'd watched all his parents and all those around him, all his life, go on and on and without. Same schedule, same events, same thoughts and feelings day after day. A gray blur, like the air above. Until finally the blur seeped into you as well, and settled there.

"We'll take it," the man said.

"Oh, darling!"

Mr. Means nodded. "I hoped you'd realize how right it is for the two of you. Saw that right away, myself." A recorder appeared. He held it half at arm's length, peering. Fingers moved on the eye. "Short term at—"

"Long term," the man said.

The woman turned her head sharply to him.

"Long term," Mr. Means said without missing a beat. "Of course. Now for that, like I brought out to you, I have to go by the book, get approval from my handler." Light touch on the eye here, little more than a brush, longer one there. Then the smile: "Course, I never was much one for the books."

Finished, Mr. Means thumbed the recorder to display mode. The man looked it over and entered his code as Mr. Means glanced discreetly away.

"Welcome home," Mr. Means said, and went out the door.

When the man turned back, his wife (he'd have to start thinking of her that way now, he reminded himself) was gone. From the bathroom, that marvelous bathroom with crumbling plaster walls, broken tiles and rust stains, he heard the toilet flush. Mr. Means had shown them how the toilet used actual water, two gallons that got filtered, purified and re-circulated again and again. There was a second flush as her clothes blew down into the vats for recycling. It sounded as though someone had held down adjacent keys on an accordion and tugged hard.

She came out after a moment and lay on the bed. Neither of them had thought to bring along new clothes; he'd have to go out later to purchase some. It had all happened so fast. But they'd heard about the apartment and rushed right over to see it. Now he'd signed away the equivalent of a full year's labor, enough to provide housing in the commons for the next ten.

Her dark hair lay long and loose on sheets that looked almost like cotton. When he sat beside her, one of the bed's bottom legs collapsed. The man and woman lurched together as though troughing a wave, and when they did, the other legs gave way as well. The man and woman laughed. With something that sounded very much like real joy.

"It's everything I could have imagined, darling," she said at length. "Everything. Oh, thank you!"

Maybe the old ways, some of them, *were* better, he told himself. Maybe we feel the way we do because we've lost all sense of tradition, all continuity. Maybe it's time for us to get some of that, what we can of it, back.

Periodically he woke to dial coffee or gruel from a console in the wall alongside the bed designed to look like an old radio. Once, he started from a dream of seas and dark skies and something coming towards him over the water.

He rose that time and stood by the window. Light had started up again by then. It swelled against the buildings, began enveloping them. Below in the alleyway he could see one of the workers peering over the top of the wall from within as the final bricks were set in place.

Later, when light had given way, had let go its hold again on buildings and sky, he lay awake still as she slept beside him. Cockroaches came out of the walls, following paths of inlaid wires, the same paths each time they appeared. Their eyes seemed to him to glow dully in the dark. He wondered if she knew they were mechanical.

Venice Is Sinking into the Sea

SHE LOVED HIM, Dana thinks, more than most, as she walks in the small park across from the house she's rented for twelve years now. A Craftsman house from the Thirties, two bedrooms, living room, kitchen, all of them much of a size. This time of morning the park's filled with the homeless. They appear each day as the sun comes up, depart each evening, trailing off into the sunset with their bedrolls, clusters of overstuffed plastic bags, shopping carts. Occasionally she wonders where it is they go. Lord, she was going to miss him.

Almost no traffic on the street where late each Friday night you can hear hot cars running against one another. Dana walks leisurely across to have coffee and a bagel at Einstein's. She knows the bagels are bogus (she's from the City, after all), but she loves them. Feels much the same way about the muscular firemen who hang out here most days.

Sean was a fireman. Smaller than most, right at the line, which meant he'd always had to work harder, do more, to make the grade. Same in bed. "I'm always humping," he'd once said, unconscious of irony. Despite his size, or because of it, he'd gone right up (as it were) the ladder, promotion after promotion. With each promotion he was less and less at home, more and more preoccupied when there beside her.

Sean was the first, messy one.

She'd never much liked Dallas anyway, and started up a new life in Boston. Brookline, actually, wherefrom she hitched rides, in those trusting, vagabond Sixties, to the library downtown. Her apartment house was up three long, zigzag terraces from the street. Furniture from salvage stores filled it, a faded leather love seat, stacked mattress and box springs, formica kitchen table standing on four splayed feet, edged with a wide band of ridged steel. Wooden chairs that seemed to have legs all of different lengths. A line of empty fishbowls.

Almost every day back then they'd be flushed out of the library because of bomb threats. There was never a bomb, just the threats, and the dogs and the bomb squad filing in. The announcement came over an intercom used for nothing else but to call closing time. Patrons would gather outside on the square (this in itself seemed so very Boston, so old America) and wait, fifteen minutes, thirty, an hour, to be allowed back in. One of those times, Will Barrett Jr. struck up a conversation with her. He was there reading up on subarachnoid hemorrhages. Couldn't get into the Mass General computers, he said, and had to evacuate one the next day. They never made it back into the library. Had moderate quantities of bad Italian food, inordinate quantities of good beer, the whole of an amazing night. She never asked how his patient had fared.

She'd hang there naked and shivering, steam banging in the radiators, twelve degrees outside (he always left the radio on), waiting for him to come home, thighs streaming with desire and the morning's deposition of semen. Because she wouldn't let herself become a victim, and because that was what he wanted, she became instead a kind of animal. Smelled it on him, another woman, one day when he came home and unlocked the cuffs. She'd learned a lot by then. That one wasn't messy.

Wayne worked at the Boston Globe, writing what they call human interest features. Roxbury woman puts three kids through college scrubbing floors, the emperor of shoeshine stands, Mister John sees the city from his front porch, that sort of thing. Most of it Wayne simply made up. Each morning four or five newspapers showed up in his driveway, the Globe, New York Times, Washington Post, Wall Street Journal, L.A. Times. He never read them. He'd sit around all day drinking beer and watching TV and after dinner he'd go into his office and tap out his column on a tan IBM Selectric. This would take an hour, tops. Then he'd call the paper. They'd send a messenger over. Wayne would join Dana to watch whatever was on at nine. Many times, the next morning, she'd be able to see in the column pieces of what they'd watched on TV in early evening. For a month, maybe two, the sex was great, then it was nonexistent. For a long time Dana didn't understand that. Then she remembered how Wayne was always grabbing something new, holding on for dear life for an hour or two, letting go. Ask him about that mother out in Roxbury and he wouldn't even remember.

Simply amazing, what you can do with a hat pin. You introduce it at the base of the skull, just under the hair line. They weren't easy to find these days, but soon, haunting antique shops, she had a collection of them. Plain hat pins, hat pins tipped with pink pearl, with abalone or plastic. Her favorite had a head with a tiny swan carved of ivory. They were amazingly long.

Jamie worked on the floor at the Chicago Stock Exchange, pushing will and voice above the crowd to move capital from here to there. He did well, but the work seemed to absorb all his energies. He came home ready and able to do little more than eat the takeout Chinese he brought and watch mindless TV—sitcoms and their like. Night after night Dana lay throbbing and alone, wondering how it had ever come about that she'd attached herself to this man.

St. Louis then, heart of the heartland, about which Dana remembered little more than the man's name, the Western shirts he favored, the look of his eyes in the mirror.

Minnesota, where for weeks at the time ice lay on the land like a solid sea and blades of wind hung spinning in the air.

New York, finally. Home. Where she thought she'd be safe with Jonas, her obscure writer who published in small magazines no one read, and should have known better. Essentially a hobbyist, she thought. Now to everyone's surprise, his more than anyone else's, Jonas is fast becoming a bestseller. His novel, written in a week, went into six printings. McSweeney's and the Times are calling him up. So tonight, after the dinner she's spent hours preparing for him, coq au vin and white asparagus with garlic butter (cookbook propped on the window ledge), a good white wine, cheese and fruit, he excuses himself "to get some writing done."

He's been writing all day.

"What are you working on?" she asks.

"Couple of things, really. That piece for Book World's almost due. And yesterday I got an idea for a new story."

Later she enters what he's dubbed The Factory, a second bedroom apparently intended for a family with a dwarf child. His desk takes up most of one wall. Two filing cabinets occupy the opposite corners, by the door, and books are stacked along the walls. Pushed back from the desk, he has the keyboard in his lap, eyes on the screen. There she sees the words "Death by misadventure."

No. By unfaithfulness, rather.

Because he loves something else more than he loves her.

She stands quietly watching. He is concentrating on the story and never realizes she's there with him. As he scrolls to the top of the screen, the title appears: "Venice Is Sinking into the Sea."

It's a story about her, of course.

She who lifts her hand now, she whose hair is so beautiful as it begins to fall.

Pitt's World

SOMETIME IN THE fourth month Pitt discovered that the small octopus-like creatures scuttling forever across the sand could be eaten. The taste was not all that unpleasant.

Stores had given out six weeks in, just before he found Diderot's body. After that Pitt subsisted on cargo. The *Bounty* was, had been, a supply ship, carrying in its hold among much else a full complement of medical supplies bound for the colonies. Bags of TPN, for instance: total parenteral nutrition. By trial and error Pitt had learned to find a vein, insert a needle and tape it in place. He walked about with the TPN bag perched on his shoulder like a mad skipper's parrot, essential nutrients dripping into his bloodstream.

By law, Class D vessels such as the *Bounty*, dedicated to routine runs with minimal crews, bore systems redundant to such extent that in effect they comprised two ships superimposed one upon the other. How it came about that piggybacked navigational and drive systems gave out simultaneously, four-in-one, Pitt had no idea. But suddenly they'd found themselves with failing power and little control—rudderless. So much for redundancy.

The *Bounty* had pulled out from Earth with the usual three-man crew.

Flight officer Waylan Diderot, a middle-aged man with hair transplants (Oriental, from the look of it), body freshly liposuctioned and sculptured, newly implanted enamel-on-steel teeth. He and Pitt had been out together at least half a dozen times.

Navigator and computer specialist Cele Gold. New to the run, but she'd done two re-ups in the Navy. Knew the why and how of it, no doubt about that, though occasionally she stumbled over the slackness and informality of civilian hopping, something that, given the chance, she'd soon have got over.

Pitt was responsible for everything else. Seeing cargo on board and safely stowed, invoices, stores, meals, permits and visas, communications. Word among merchant marines was that no better petty officer could be had. Pitt showed no pride at that. He'd fallen into the work by chance after leaving the seminary in his final year when, sitting over his bowl of tea one early morning, watching light gather outside, it came to him that he believed none of it. He was never able to summon any regret at this sudden loss of faith—more a recognition of its absence than a loss, actually. He'd simply stepped through a door, into a new room. He would have been a decent, unremarkable priest. Now he was a first-rate petty officer.

Only once had the old life reared its head into the present. Following an exceptionally long flight, having finally delivered their cargo, Pitt and his F.O. sat in a bar pickling themselves on the local distillate.

"God can't find us here," the F.O. said.

Every bit as blasted as his flight officer, Pitt asked: "Why would he be looking?"

"According to the religious, he always is. Eye on the sparrow and all that? Back home, as a young man—more years ago than I wish to think about—I believed. Out here, I no longer have to."

"Perhaps," Pitt said after a moment, "you have recovered your innocence."

They'd all been cross-trained, of course. Not that it mattered now. In a pinch any of the three of them could pilot the ship, run new programs and protocols, lift off, set down, punch in coordinates and routing sequences.

Problem was, the training assumed you had a functional ship.

Moments before alarms sounded, Diderot had bellowed out:

"What the fuck!" Then: "Cele?"

"I know, I know. Can't get a fix on it. . . . Auxiliaries are kicking in, but they're at maybe sixty per cent, at best. Navigational's gone—"

"Pitt?"

"Not much better at this station, I'm afraid, sir."

"—and there goes the backup right after it."

"Distress signal?"

"Affirmative. I'm trying to run a tracer. . . . Both keep getting bounced back."

"Maybe no one's home," Diderot said.

They were all thinking the same thing. War had been brewing for some time, and seemed imminent as they lifted. Perhaps it had erupted. Perhaps, for now, they were completely, utterly on their own.

"Shit! Communications just went down, sir."

As did they.

In situations like this, even at low function, the ship followed a lifeline scenario: located the nearest land, lashed onto it, reeled itself in. Within minutes they were looking out at tall, slender trees bearded with what appeared to be moss and studded with pads of yellow fungus like hobnails on boots. The trees rose not from soil but from sand, or its equivalent. Small, octopuslike creatures by the dozens scuttled across it.

"Everyone okay?"

"Yeah."

"Me too, though I think 'okay' just took on a new meaning. Where the hell are we?"

"Off the charts, sir."

"Well, doesn't *that* surprise us."

"Atmosphere's oxygen-heavy—"

"No wonder, all those trees."

"—but serviceable."

Remaining ship systems were shutting down one by one. A pale sun hung half below the horizon, giving light. Dawn? Dusk? For all they knew, it might be there all the time.

Cele was first to hit the button. Her spidery harness withdrew, and she stood, going up on the balls of her feet, down, back up.

"Just lost about twenty pounds," she announced. "Crash diet."

They both groaned.

"Permission to recon, sir?" Cele asked.

"Be careful out there."

Slinging a survival pack over one shoulder, she touched a finger to forehead in salute and hit the slide, sinking quickly from sight. Pitt and Diderot watched on monitors as she exited the ship, moving off into the trees.

They never saw her again.

Five and a half weeks after that, 0800 ship's time—unlike the F.O. to remain abed, he was thinking—Pitt entered captain's quarters. Diderot lay in repose and at peace on the steel cot that folded up into the wall. His handheld sat at bedside, cursor blinking. A message to his wife.

I know you'll never see this, my dear Val. Like so many utterances, it's more for my own benefit than for anyone else. Seems I've come to the end of all these strange roads I've chosen. But God, we had some good years, didn't we! Here (I almost wrote "Where I've fallen to earth") there's little to sustain life, far less to sustain hope. The last things I will see and feel are your face and your love. I've known that for a long time now. Even if I tried again and again and could never say how very much you meant to me.

Pitt saw to it that Diderot got a decent burial. TPN bag balanced on his shoulder, he said a few words over the grave as the small octopus-like creatures skittered across the newly disturbed sand, said things about Diderot being a good man and being missed, though he couldn't imagine the creatures much cared. He finished: Requiescat in pace. That was the day he began thinking of where he now lived as *Pace*.

2.

THE CREATURES SCUTTLING about the sand came in an array of colors though the majority of them tended towards light green and a sort of aqua. Darker ones seemed frequently to be attacked and destroyed by their neighbors. About the time he started harvesting them, Pitt had begun to wonder if perhaps they, or at least some among them, possessed the capacity to change color. They had a thin skin that, given a shallow slit, was easily peeled away. The flesh beneath was pulpy, white. With minutes over an open fire it became tender.

To support a food chain, there had to be other fauna. Pitt knew that but came across no evidence of same. He did find a variety of edible leaves and a tasty, somewhat bitter root. Tossed into the pot together with the small creatures, these gave up not only a nice stew but essential roughage as well.

Near where he'd set up camp ran a wide, shallow stream populous with fish that seemed to be all the same species. Resembling nothing so much as a child's ballet slippers, they were transparent, one with the water. But when they turned, light caught somewhere in their bodies, and for that moment they became iridescent, spilling color after color, in pools, into the water about them.

Pitt often thought how much easier things could have been if only the computer had survived. Then he might have acquired crucial knowledge and skills: water purification, essentials of medicine, principles of architecture, basic carpentry, soap making.

Robinson Crusoe and his parasol. Pitt and his soap rendered from the fat of the octopus-like creatures. Scented perhaps with blooms from one or another of the local blooms.

As a civilized man, city born and bred, Pitt knew nothing of any of this—means to safe water, medicine—least of all something like soap making, so very many *more* giant steps into the past. Why he thought he needed such information never quite came clear to him. Just that he was convinced he should know those things.

Truly, though, Pitt's new home gave him all he needed.

One handheld, solar-powered like the ship's clock, did function intermittently. He should save that for an emergency, he decided—then laughed. *Emergency* had certainly taken on a different meaning.

The sound of his laughter startled him. And was as close to Friday's footprints as he ever came.

In one out-of-the-way cabinet of what remained of the ship—most of the corpse had been taken over by vegetation now—he found a survival kit. The kit consisted of a week's supply of nutrient capsules, water-purification tablets, basic tools, self-propelling nails and bolts, fishing line, a mess kit, a spark generator, an ingenious sheet, thin as foil, that could double as blanket or tent, flares the size of firecrackers, a first-aid kit, a handgun, a distress beacon.

It took him over a month, ship's time, to get the beacon working, but by trial and error and doggedness he did, managing to hook depleted batteries extracted from various backup systems and small appliances together in series, tapping and collectivizing their residual charges. (Ship's time was all he had, of course. Though maybe it would be closer to the truth to hold that time had ceased to matter at all—and so had ceased to exist.) The beacon's tiny red active light, when it came on, seemed to him far brighter than the sun hanging motionless, another token of time's suspension, half below the horizon.

For all Pitt's good intentions, soon enough he was playing chess with the solar-powered handheld. After all, there was so little to occupy him here. One could spend only so many hours and days staring off into the trees, one could eat only so many meals, one could sleep only so many hours. With each move, he knew, he was draining the handheld's reserve. But what else was there?

Disappointingly, and more quickly then he'd anticipated, the handheld went from winning each game to shutting down with games barely started.

So, what now?

Any major fauna beyond the octopus-like creatures still eluded him, but a rough equivalent of insects existed in profusion. Most of these were by Pitt's standards large, ranging from roughly hummingbird- to sparrow-size; all, as far as he could tell, were flightless. He began collecting them, pinning them to a bulletin board of cork he'd ransomed from the *Bounty*. Each specimen bore the specifics of its collection. Ship's date, ship's time, location. *5-5-21, four clicks starboard, sector G-19-N.*

He had no means of preserving the specimens, of course. (Something else he might have learned from the lapsed computers.) Before his very eyes, he knew, the collection would disintegrate. Vestigial wings fall off, exoskeletons crumble, till finally there'd be little more than a whisper of dust left at the base of the pins. But for now his collection was definitive.

Definitely world's best, he thought.

What impelled people towards collecting in the first place? A strange occupation. Some inborne drive for hunting and gathering pushed forward to the point there was no longer any need for same, so that it broke out, bespoke itself, in new forms? Or something closer to the ground? I have more bones ivory gold stamps coins than you. I win.

So much of life, so much of society, was competition. Pitt, alone as few had ever been alone, stood apart from all that now, in a kind of innocence.

He had seen Diderot through to a decent burial, he'd searched for Cele, there was little left to do. He spent his days arranging his collection of insects according to color, according to order of discovery, according to size.

It occurred to him that this was in itself only another kind of chess.

3.

AMONG CELE'S SPARE personal possessions, Pitt found a book to which he'd have paid little attention were it not for its title: *Peace*. He'd never been much of a reader and couldn't in fact recall when he'd last held a book.

Peace. *Pace.*

Subtitled "A Novel in Verse," the book related the epic struggle between two diverse cultures living on either side of a river, on twin narrow strips of arable land beyond which stretched seemingly endless desert. The inside flap bore a photograph of a young man of indeterminate ethnicity. The title page was inscribed "To Cele—We'll always have Memphis" and signed by the author.

Maybe it was only that the book afforded him some sense of community, a vision or momento of the civilization he'd left behind, at first willfully, now by mischance and (it would certainly seem) finally. Before, he'd have had no interest in reading anything like this. But since finding it he had been through the book so many times that he could recite whole pages by heart.

The sun's bead drew out to a thin line. The sharks
were hungry that year, the days made of wood.
In the loftiest vaults they could find, birds turned straw
to the gold of new birth, nervously eyeing the horizon.
While in every lit doorway stood dark figures. . . .

On the day he'd first eaten one of the octopus-like creatures, thinking that he had no idea what poisons or deadly bacteria could lurk within them, or how simply inimical might be their tissue to his own, Pitt lay down half- expecting to die, perhaps in truth half-hoping for it. He rose surprised to find himself not only alive but revitalized. This world had accepted him; he was a part of it now. On *Pace.* At peace.

Today he has been sitting for some time, or for no time, on the bank of the stream. And when at last he rises, it's to retrieve the distress beacon and throw it into the stream. The ship's clock goes next. Briefly, water alive with color, pool after pool of bright green, chrome yellow, purple, scarlet, the fish swarm about these new, strange things that have suddenly entered their world. Then, turning, all but invisible again, they move on.

Flesh of Stone and Steel

THERE WAS STILL water in the canals then. Waiting for you to come home, I had little else to do, and spent hours by it. Amazing how sensuous water can be, turning within itself, carressing the flanks of the shore, catching light and playing with it, throwing it back. Around one slow turn, as the canal contorted to fit itself to what remained of downtown, people sat outdoors drinking coffee at a small café at all hours, coats drawn close about them, breaths stabbing horse tails into the air. Behind layers of gauzelike exhausted air, the sun, paler than any moon, struggled to be seen.

O my love. I saw you in them all. In water's play, in the gay waiter's hips as he sashayed among tables, in every defeated, expectant face. Were the café there now, I've no doubt I would find you still. I've been back. Indifferent piles of stone where the front wall was pushed down or collapsed of its own unsupported weight, a scatter of smashed tables and crippled chairs, algae grown over the lip of the tiny fountain in a spill and become something else, something like grass, seeking reproduction by whatever means necessary, at any cost, any measure, life that will not be stopped.

At night I'd lie looking across your ravaged body to the window, remembering a time when cities had been things of light, almost alive themselves.

That last winter, perched hawklike in your thirteenth-floor loft above the dissolving city, I wrote my first and finest poems. Sometimes now I wonder just how those came about. Incredible that they did. Since then there've been few, fewer still of any note.

I also wrote dozens of fragments like the following, strange conjunctions of mind and external world that came to nothing and were soon abandoned. Fragments, I suppose, because that's what my life was, what all our lives were.

THE THEATRE IS in blackness.

Voice #1: *At first, everything is in darkness. Light begins slowly.*

Right on cue, light does so, and gradually we discern the outlines of a stage set, of two people. The woman stands at a window rear stage, back to us. We assume it is a woman. The man sits on a couch stage left; from time to time he jots something into a notebook on his lap. Music is playing. We assume it is music. An assemblage of sounds, at any rate.

Voice #2: *Autumn. The city remains under seige. Past their indow it lies, a luminous landscape of swells and hollows, like the body of a woman done with desire.*

Woman: *There are fires everywhere. Everything is burning. The past is almost gone now, I think.*

Man (listening): *So exquisite. Could we hear it again, do you think?*

Back still turned, the woman crosses the stage to a bank of apparatus, meters, gauges. The music stops, then starts back up.

Woman: *Would you like tea?*

Man: *Love a cup.*

Woman: *There's a bit of bread left as well. Frightfully stale, I'm afraid: I'd have to toast it.*

Man: *Then by all means do, my dear.*

The woman crosses the stage again. Stands at a counter stage right as she puts on the kettle, slices bread, rummages noisily for silverware, plates, cups.

Woman (working): *Do you remember the day we first met?*

Man: *Of course.*

Woman: *It all happened so fast. I'd never felt anything like this before.*

The man gets up and walks to her. They stand together looking out an imaginary window above the counter.

Woman: *I'm so cold. So very cold.*

I NEVER KNEW when you would come. You had lives elsewhere, and for days, a week or more, once for over a month, you'd be gone, then just as suddenly and unpredictably there when I returned from the café, from the river, from hours passed prowling streets as silent witness. Opening at my approach, the door would tell me matter-of-factly: *Cat is here.*

The addicted person, you said, can no longer distinguish between his pleasure and his pain. That border, that threshhold, is gone. Others soon follow, in sequence.

That was what you did in your days and nights and weeks away from me, you worked with them, tried to help them understand and to understand them, people with something of the heroic in them, people at once larger than life and caricatures of a kind, shrunken to the smallest common denominator of desire, of need. Their numbers grew daily in our shadow world beneath the media's blinding white light and a dimming sun, where it was forever late afternoon, early evening.

Tell me what it is like, you said one morning, to have someone that close, that joined, that much a part of you.

I tried, and couldn't.

Was it from your despair, from your identification with them, that you joined those you couldn't help? Maybe if you better understood, you *would* be able to help. Maybe if you shared their suffering, your own would be diminished.

As I suppose, in some manner, it was.

I could not cut you out of me, I said that day. You are a part of my flesh.

Now I watch the city continue becoming flame and remember the intense white flame that was you. All about me fire's harsh red head tears up from the city's ruins, all about me it puts out tender hands, touching, teasing, fire that knows my name, fire that wants me, cold fire that will have us all.

Up

TWO WENT UP on the bus today. One was an elderly lady who came aboard at the stop near Megaworld with her collapsible rolling cart and sat huddled for close to half an hour in blue bundle of skirt, sweater and what she'd no doubt have called a wrap. Then she took a sigh and went up. The other was a young man pierced all about, ears, nose, tongue, eyebrow, as though to provide rings and hitches by which he might be lashed to the world. His eyes were never still. Ten blocks into his ride he stood and let out a scream of rage or challenge, a single burst, like a flare, before he went up. The rest of us watched a moment, then went about our business. For most of us, of course, our business isn't much. I've read that when the bomb was dropped on Hiroshima, people's shadows were burned onto walls. That's what the tracings always remind me of, those faint outlines of gray like photographs that haven't quite been captured, the bare footprints of ash, left behind when they go up.

When these two went up, I was, first, just beginning, then four hours into, my daily countdown, carrying on the shabby pretense that things were as they'd always been or soon would be again, yoyoing in dark suit, pinpoint oxford shirt and briefcase uptown, crosstown, downtown and back, filling out applications here, dropping off a resume there, but mostly sitting on park benches and on buses like this one. Go through the motions, people tell you, and form becomes content. Keep putting the vessel out and it'll fill. As usual people, the ones who give you advice anyway, are full of shit.

The curious thing is that there's no heat when they go up.

Mrs. Lancaster-Smith appeared on the landing as I climbed past her floor. Four more to go, thousands of us all over the city making the same or some similar climb now in suit, overalls, casual dresses, workclothes and jeans, coming home. "You forgot to lock up again," she said. Her voice pursued me up the stairs the way squeaky bedsprings carry through apartment walls. "Mr. Abib, from the next floor down?, was out on the landing, having a cup of whatever that is he drinks all the time, that always smells so sweet?, and heard voices. He walked up and found two kids standing outside your door. Another couple were on their way in." I thanked her and said I would be more careful, thinking all the time that *forgot* probably wasn't the correct word. At one level or another I was probably hoping someone would go in and strip everything out, carry off every trace of my previous life, give me permission to start over.

I climbed on, unlocked the door and went in. The logbox in the corner of the screen opposite the door registered four calls, three pieces of mail, a couple of bills paid as of nine this morning. "Hello, Annette," I said. *I'm home*, I thought. The screen itself showed prospects of blue sky, white clouds moving through them calm and slow as glaciers.

She'd gone up sixteen days before. We were sitting on a bench by the river downtown, the river they'd spent so much controversial taxpayer's money building. A plaque on the back of the bench read The Honorable Lawrence Block. All the benches were named for Senators who, having called in favors to finance creation of the river, couldn't leverage further funds from the House and finally elected to pay for benches, walkways and riverside amenities personally. Annette and I had had dinner at a Vietnamese restaurant, huge bowls of soup into which we threw sprigs of cilantro and mint, dollops of hot sauce, sprouts, then gone for a walk. The sunset was splendid, as it is most days now, sunsets being dependent upon such things as pollution indexes, dust and particle content. We sat watching as clouds filled with pink, as purple began seeping up like a dark, beautiful ink off the horizon, staining the sky.

"I'm so happy," Annette said beside me. I'd brought along a cup of Vietnamese coffee laced with condensed milk. I had it halfway to my mouth when she went up.

Then there was only that faint gray outline of a body on the bench beside me, that bare footprint of ash. After a moment, I drank.

"Hungry?" I said now, coming into the apartment. "I'm starved." Hard day at the office and all that. God knows why, but I'd gone on talking to her all this time. I came home, asked about her day, poured two glasses of wine, chatted as I cooked. This is what people, what couples, families, did. They made the climb in suit, overalls, casual dresses, workclothes or jeans. They came home, inquired after the children, asked how the day had gone, if there had been any calls. Sometimes the meals I fixed were inspired. Often they were commonplace, barely edible; I could never discern what made the difference. Sometimes when I spoke to Annette, confused as to whom I might be addressing, the computer tried to respond.

The parent chosen for me by lottery was Mimi Blodgett: a name that, when I first heard it, made me wonder if I'd not somehow fallen through cracks in reality's pavement directly into a Dickens novel. But no, that was indeed her name, and she lived up to it. A barrel-shaped woman, foreshortened everywhere, arms, legs, neck, intellect; hair dyed brown and set each week at Josie's Cool Fixin's, Friday, 3 P.M., in curls that defied not only age but gravity as well; an armory of polyester pants, shirtwaists and pullovers in the rickety closet, stacks of Reader's Digests in the bathroom, of her trailer. Mimi's love for me was like that trailer, never intended to be permanent though it turned out that way, and as durable basically (if also as unlovely and plain) as her rack of polyester. She worked at Billy's, the local drugstore, stocking shelves, hauling boxes out of the backs of trucks, helping at the register when once or twice a week, mostly Fridays, things got busy. She'd bring home discontinued merchandise for me, packets of candy, cheese crackers and Christmas toys initially (including a submarine that, spoonful of baking soda tamped into ballast tank, sank and rose, sank and rose), later on shaving lather, razors, cheap aftershave I told her was perfect and never used.

It took her a long time to die. None of those hundreds of movies and stories tell you how long it can take people to die, and none give you any idea how death smells, the sweat that soaks into sheets and mattress and won't be expunged, the ever-present tang of urine, blossom of alcohol over it all, earthy, garden smell of feces under. Dying people themselves begin to stink. They stink in ways that go far beyond the unmistakeable, sweetish smell, a smell you never forget, of the cancer itself. They know this: you can see it in their eyes. Towards the end you see little else there. The sickness is eating its way out of their body, like an insect. They've *become* the sickness. And so, for a while, as caretaker, do you. As all the while, leaving us, they rise higher and higher, air ever thinning.

The best part of the day was always when we came home, that first hour or two. Annette wrote code for an insurance company, I wrote advertising copy. Our arrivals never varied more than ten minutes. This was before I switched to buses, when I still took the sub-t, and sometimes we'd come up from opposite ends of the station simultaneously, pink flowers with dark stems blooming from the ground. We'd walk the six blocks to our apartment, I'd loosen my tie, she'd slip out of her shoes. And we'd sit there, young professionals in grownup clothes, part of the glue that held it all together, two people very much *in the world* as Heidegger would say, over glasses of wine and eventually, maybe along about the second glass, a plate of cheese and olives.

Thing is, no glue holds forever, and once Annette was gone, veneers started peeling away everywhere: I saw the world's furniture for the shoddy goods it was. Shortly thereafter I began to notice how many were going up.

They'd been doing this for some time, of course; I knew that. I'd just never taken much notice. It had little to do with me, after all, little to do with *my* life of gourmet coffee, clients, spreadsheets, presentations. Packaging is what I was about, what I did: my genius, if you will. *Another sort of veneer*, I thought at first with Annette's departure—then realized it was in fact far more central. I had been instrumental in helping create nothing less than a new language, a house of words and image that, progressively, we'd all moved into to live. And now we couldn't get out.

Having realized this, I began to stutter. No longer could I begin sentences effectively or find my way easily to the end of them. Glibness, once gone, rarely can be regained.

The first one I witnessed go up was during *The Barber of Seville*. We'd bought season tickets almost a year back when life was casually on course, glibness intact, and $480 didn't have to be thought about; the tickets, at least, were still good. Ah, sweet irony. I couldn't pay my rent, but I could attend the opera. Sat there with the empty chair next to me fuller than most, watching beautiful women file in fawning over men in ugly coats and ties.

In the row behind me, six seats down, one of these men repeatedly fell asleep, to be, at first, whispered, then, irritation growing, elbowed awake by his companion. Said companion wore a gown artfully contriving to push her sagging bosom back towards cleavage and conceal a thickening middle. His suit, by contrast, had come right off the rack, coat 44, slacks 40x32, and was cinched like a saddle by a Western belt, its buckle the size of demitasse saucers and so shiny that lasers might have been bounced off it.

Halfway into the first act, Rosina pondering the voice she's heard below her balcony, the woman prised him awake for the fifth, sixth time.

He came round groggily this time, slow to surface, to come to knowledge where he was. He looked at his companion for a moment with brimming eyes, took a deep sigh, and went up.

Those in seats close by leaned away from the sudden, intense light and coughed apologetically.

Another empty seat then, like the one beside me. As this silliest of the great operas rolled on.

That evening, *après* opera, I created a sauce of porcini mushrooms, stock, red wine and roux, serving it over fresh polenta. I ate my own portion slowly, with half a bottle of a good Chardonnay, then scraped Annette's into the disposal. She had little appetite these days. Someday soon, I suspected, my own would fail. Afterwards I retrieved a favorite volume of Montaigne from the shelf and settled into bed with same, but found myself unable or unwilling to follow the scurry of his mind from notion to notion—the very quality for which I revered him.

On the bus the next morning I found my gaze drawn back again and again from observation of the world about me—drawn back, that is, from simple witness of those waiting at curbside and the ones who clambered aboard, corpuscles streaming through the city carrying nutrients and oxygen, keeping it alive—to billboards set in place above the train's windows. The windows themselves were scored amateurishly, tags and incomprehensible messages scratched roughly into them. While, above, pros had *their* say. Public service announcements, some, for clinics and the like, and in a variety of languages. The bulk of them, however, were ads of one sort or another, samples of that dialect, the idiom of American commerce, that's rapidly becoming our only language. Like any other native tongue, we learn it without direct intent, simply by exposure, absorbing it; after which, it governs not only the way we think, but what we're able to think.

I became silent that day. Not with the silence of Quakers, opening a space for whatever voice might come into it, God's perhaps, or that of my own conscience; nor with Gandhian silence, adopted in the knowledge that utterance itself is a kind of action, all action a species of violence; rather, with a silence akin to the silence of the world itself, and that of the things within it. I spoke only when necessary, only when there was information, *real* information, needing communication—that kind of silence. A silence all but lost to the murderous din of our materialism. As though if there were not this continuous noise, there would be nothing to hold us up, nothing for us to stand upon.

That day, as well, I began keeping a notebook in which I recorded all I could discover about those who went up in my presence. Often the page held little more than date, time and place. Occasionally a fact or two some momentary neighbor could recall when questioned: where the client came aboard the bus, what the client had carried with him. Upon occasion, comments from a driver who remembered the client from previous days. Sometimes, if I had nothing else, a sketch: stick figures ensconced in rear seats; bundles left behind.

Suddenly, then, it was fall. One morning, having come out in suit and tie as usual, I looked around in surprise at fellow passengers in coats and, as they stepped from the heated bus stop into that small band of open world before boarding the bus, the plumes of their breath. People had bulked up in dark colors; each leaf on each tree was a different blend of brown, yellow, red, rust, cinnamon, gold. Winds flew like great, silent birds through the caverns and canyons of the city.

That evening I sat in my apartment with Jorge, who brought with him a twelve-pack of South African beer. Jorge was virtually the only friend I had left. I'd run off the others, who grew tired (though a few, from loyalty or brute force of will, clung on till the end) first of reminiscences of Annette, then of unending discourse on this thing one did not speak of, all those going up around us. We were watching a movie I'd dialed in on the phone line, a Chinese comedy whose tags and markers were absolutely impenetrable to us. From time to time Jorge or I laughed, looking to the other to see if possibly we'd guessed correctly. An hour or so in, I set it on pause and did a quick stir-fry: carrots, celery, apple, tofu, lots of soy sauce. Rice being in short supply that month, I served it over couscous.

We moved onto the balcony to eat. Said balcony comprised a scant yard or so of floorspace extended out from the apartment and cut off by railings, of which the rental agents were nonetheless inordinately proud. Whenever I went out there, I felt I'd been set to walk the plank.

Jorge was never much for talking. We'd sat together through entire evenings during which he released, like bubbles floating slowly to the surface, perhaps a total of ten words. My own conversation, predictably enough, soon swerved from discussion of the movie (there was little enough to discuss, after all) to the folks I'd seen go up recently. Jorge nodded from time to time. Then, miraculously, he spoke.

"There's never a morning I don't wake up thinking about it, wondering if this is the day I'll finally get down and do it. You want to know why I never have?" He took a swig of his beer. The label was all bright colors and zigzags, like a poisonous snake. "Cause I look like shit in gray, man." He laughed. "Besides, anyone hauls my ashes, it's gonna be me, you know?"

This from a man I would have considered the most undisturbed, the most untouchable (if also, or likewise, the most unimaginative), I knew. Scratch the veneer of a life, anyone's life, I suppose, and there's little beneath but cheap wood or pressboard, pain, despair.

No wonder they go up so fast.

Jorge and I never got back to the movie. We sat wordlessly there on the balcony as buses stopped running, as one by one streetlights and lights in all but government, emergency and residential buildings went out.

"Best get along," Jorge said.

Together we looked down towards the city's dark floor, far below.

"What about curfew?"

My friend shrugged. "It's a short walk. Skin like mine, who's to see me? I'm a moving shadow."

"You could stay over."

"Course I could. But you out of beer, man."

I smiled, immediately wondering when I'd last done so. "Take care, my friend."

He left without responding, without any show of leavetaking as always; part of that silence of the world and its things that I'd come to embrace; I suppose this was why I so valued his company. I gathered up dishes, bottles, utensils, took the movie off pause and shut it down, swished and gargled mouthpaste, smeared on cleanser and, looking in the mirror, wiped it off.

"Goodnight, Annette," I said quietly.

This was one of the times the computer grew confused.

"Excuse me."

"Yes?"

"Would you please repeat your last command?"

Realizing what had happened, I told it to delete.

"Are you sure?"

"Yes."

"Good night, then."

The next morning I slept late. Near noon, still in jeans and sweatshirt reading *What? Me Hurry?* I went down into the street. I had no intimations of higher directives, no wisdom, to bring down to them. Not anymore. I was done with all that. But I could join them in their sadness and pain.

At the Cheyenne Diner two blocks up, where occasionally I had breakfast, less occasionally dinner, I sat on a red-upholstered stool at the counter, as always, and attempted to draw the man seated next to me into conversation. With the first couple of remarks, on weather and a purported loosening of the curfew as I recall, he grunted or nodded non-committally. Then, when I persisted, he glanced at me strangely. So did, in train, the waitress Maria and (I'm reasonably sure) the cook mounted at his console behind the pass-through, fingers poised over keys.

Next I progressed to the bus stop. Here, again, they all regarded me strangely: a surrogate mother with child slung between sagging breasts, two gentlemen in the orange uniforms of city sanitation, another in the pink uniform indicating a prisoner released to day work, a handful of hangers-on, outriders, in the current frontier gear of snug unbleached canvas pants, white rayon poet's shirt, Chinese cloth shoes. At the sub-t stop I'd frequented for so many years when Annette and I were together, the situation was little different. A different clientele, but that same strange regard. And much the same response to overtures of conversation.

When had people stopped talking to one another?

Entering the apartment, I stood for a moment before the screen, watching those familiar prospects of blue sky and white clouds roll across, as though a tiny portion of what used to be called *the heavens* had been caged here.

"I'm home," I said.

Choosing this occasion for discernment, the computer paused before responding. "You are addressing me?"

"Yes."

"Excellent. Would it be appropriate for me to remark that you are home early?"

"Listen. People are giving up, people everywhere. They look around them and just . . . let go. Go up, we call it."

"These people are no longer alive, you mean."

"They no longer even exist."

"I see. Why are they doing this? Or—to employ the second-person plural, as would be appropriate in such an instance—why are *you* doing this?"

"I don't know."

"Who does know?"

After a moment, when I said no more, the computer asked: "Will there be anything else?" and when still I failed to respond, shut itself down.

Leaving me suspended there in eternal mid-morning.

Day stretched out before me glacierlike, a white, featureless plain. No end to it, to any of it. Stepping out onto the balcony, from this posthistoric cave onto the cliff, I had a sudden flash, whether of intuition or some form of daydream terror I've no idea. I saw myself alone in absolute silence, all the others gone, surrounded by shelf after shelf of notebooks, hundreds upon hundreds of them, thousands, looming about me: all that remained of what had once been my race, my species, my people, mankind.

Day's Heat

WITH A LIGHT knock, she stepped into the room. Like everyone else's, even those of nurses and doctors who should be used to it by now, her eyes went first to the corner of the room.

She looked older. Fourteen years has a way of doing that. I said I was glad she came, I didn't know if she would.

"Neither did I."

Now, finally, her eyes went to the bed.

I thought: What you see is what you get. It never is, of course. "He's hanging on."

Dan stepped out from behind me. "Until you could get here, perhaps."

I thought of the strings of lies and half-truths running behind our days, holding them up. How hard we work to try to give some shape to it all.

She nodded to Dan. He nodded back. Their eyes never met.

"How bad is it? Does he even know I'm here?"

I shrugged. In the corner something happened. A new shape, a budlike swelling, ambiguous as the rest, broke through the pale white surface. If you hadn't caught the motion, you might never know anything had changed.

"Your flight okay?" I said.

"I decided to drive at the last minute."

"You'll stay with us, of course," Dan said.

"I've taken a room not far from here."

"This isn't a very safe part of town," I said. Hospitals seem always to be in the seediest sections. Out the window I had watched drug deals go down. Homeless people smeared with what looked like tar lived in the bus stop at the corner.

"It's not a very safe world."

Not that she wasn't used to it. She'd been a cop in Atlanta, what, eleven years now? Kind of life I couldn't imagine. I scarcely left the house except when Dan and I went shopping. Everything else—news, movies, work assignments—crawled in and out on the web.

"How's Larson? And the kids?"

For a moment she didn't answer. She'd look away from the corner, then her eyes would get pulled back.

"The kids are fine. Larson hasn't been around for a while now."

"I'm sorry."

"So was he."

"I guess we haven't stayed in touch very well."

She looked at me for a moment before speaking. "Why would we want to?"

Why indeed. I tried for words, but as so often out here in the world they failed me, wore false faces, masks, didn't live up to their promises or never came by at all. "It's just us now," I said finally.

From her look, that was the stupidest thing she'd ever heard anyone say. From her perspective I suppose it was.

She went to the bed and took his hand. It was impossibly white, like the inside of a mushroom. His face turned in her direction when she said his name: that was all. I thought I remembered a time when he could see, even speak a little, but maybe I imagined that. It was all years ago. For a long time now he'd been closed up inside his mind, marooned there. Except for us, of course. The Frog Prince.

Lesley stood looking down.

"So here you are, you little fuck. Everyone tells me you're dying."

She bent over him. Held-in tears slicked her eyes.

"Good," she said.

Behind me, Dan cleared his throat. "Think I'll go for a walk," he said.

The computer at which I'd been working when she came in sat blinking on a rollaway bed table. I turned it off, listening to the brief dynamo-like whine. The screen went blank.

Blank like the window. Though there, outside light made of it a brilliant backlit screen. It looked like a sheet of ice, white as this thing in the room's corner that seemed somehow to be taking the Frog Prince's place, this thing that had taken over the corner already—as he steadily diminished.

"Good," Lesley said again.

I DON'T KNOW when it first may have occurred to us that we were somehow different, that others did not live quite as we did. That they could not. As a child, whatever events take place day to day seem normal; you can hardly suspect otherwise. There's an appropriate word, *parallax*—for the way an object's position seems to change when viewed from a new line of sight. Perspective is everything.

We assumed our situation to be the way of the world, Lesley and I, and spoke freely of it between ourselves. Only later, remarks to teachers and schoolmates having made them regard us strangely, did we begin slowly (slowly, though we ceased such remarks at once) to understand that they had no conception of our home life. This realization brought the two of us still closer.

We were quite the pair those days, never apart. Read the same books, became hungry at the same time, woke within moments of one another. Had, for all I know, the same thoughts.

"Lawrence, Lesley, come along," Father would say as he collected us from the backyard where we loved, most of all, to sit in the cool shade and smell of the grape arbor, sunlight dappling us with shadowy hands. We would see who could hold a grape in his mouth the longest without biting into it. "Don't be selfish, now. Your brother needs you."

Lesley, sighing, would give me the look that said: The Frog Prince has called. For so many years we went along agreeably, never questioning, never holding back. And when finally we did, or, rather, Lesley did, we discovered just how insistent Father could become, and just how desperate was little Jamie's, the Frog Prince's, need for us.

"Help me, Larry!" Lesley cried that first time. She had refused to come along, despite Father's entreaties. Then her eyes went suddenly wild and her head slammed against the floor, back arching as convulsions began. Minutes later, wordlessly, spent, she rose and walked towards Jamie's room. I followed. It would be a long time, years, before she again offered resistance. As she stepped into sunlight from a window that day, saliva glistened on her cheek and chin. She made no move to wipe it away. It looked, I remember thinking, like ice.

REMAINS OF A dinner Dan had spent much of the afternoon preparing sat about on various surfaces: folding tables, extra chairs, the edge of the grill, flat-topped rocks, bare ground alongside. Dan did everything about the house. Cooked, cleaned, saw to it that bills got paid, repairs made, my computer files put or kept in order. Periodically I felt a certain guilt at not pulling my weight. But this is what our lives, all our lives, are about, accommodations of one sort or another. Dan was the functional part of me, the border where world and self met. In reflective moments (these occurred seldom enough) I wondered how I would ever be able to get along in the world without him. Now he'd gone off, ostensibly to prepare coffee and straighten up in the kitchen.

"Get enough?"

"Back in Atlanta, what we *didn't* eat tonight would last me a week."

"Probably do the same for us. Dan got a bit carried away." A bit. Salmon, grilled tomatoes, fresh-baked pita, two fruit salads, tiny cucumber sandwiches. "He still wants you to like him."

"It's not personal."

Out over the nearest hill a hawk banked, late light disappearing into the blackness of its wings. Three geckoes clung motionless to the window beside the back door, bodies curled into gentle crescents.

"I know it's not," I told my sister.

"Does he?"

I shook my head.

She sat peering beneath the canopy we'd constructed of tent poles and drapery remnants at the house's western edge. Neat rows of tomatoes, beans, peppers.

"I wouldn't have thought you'd be able to grow much of anything here."

"It does take work. Dan put in two years before he saw any results at all. Calls it his victory garden."

She looked at the bare, eternally dry ground about us, then to the hills with their scattered growth of hedgehog and pincushion cactus, prickly pear, cholla looking as though it should be growing beneath the sea instead of here. Halfway up, the saguaros began, time's sentinels, arms upraised. In warning, I always wondered, as if to say: go back!—or merely to get our attention? Sunlight flattened against the sky in nebulae of bright oranges, impossible blues, brilliant yellows. The day would end splendidly, as they mostly did here.

"Why on earth would anyone move to this godforsaken place?" Lesley said.

"I swore that whatever happened in my life, wherever I went, I'd never have to smell magnolias again. That sickly sweetness, and the whole town reeking of something like wet animal fur when it rained."

"And it rained every day."

"Seemed to, at least."

"Here it just looks like God squatted down, farted, and lit a match to the whole of it. Everything's brown."

"But I love the feel of space all around me. Never knew there could be so much sky. Or these incredible sunsets. And when storms come, they arrive magnificently. Lightning dances on mile-high legs. You watch it all sail in from miles and miles away." Thinking of something I'd once written: that our minds repeat the landscape.

Dan emerged with coffee thermos, cups, spoons, sugar and cream on a tray. If no one needed anything else just now, he said, then he'd get started at finding the kitchen again. It was under there somewhere.

We sipped at our coffee. One of the geckoes suddenly dashed up the length of the window to snag a moth battering at the top edge, sat working its jaws.

"We had a right to our childhood," Lesley said after a while.

I nodded. Of course we did, and both knew it. But we knew also that it was she who was the wizard of regret, the banker of anger and pain. I'd never been much good at any of it.

After a moment I motioned, and when she assented, poured more coffee for us both. Neither of us added sugar or milk. We sat quietly looking up into the hills as day faded around us.

"Maybe we don't have a right to anything," I said finally. "Maybe it all has to be wrested from the grip of something else: our lives, who we are—even a pleasant day's end like this one. Maybe it's best that we recognize that, learn to get along without all the stories that reassure us, make us comfortable."

"Jesus. *Now* I feel better. Thanks, little brother." She laughed. I remembered that laugh. Years ago. "Same cheerful goddamned son of a bitch you always were, aren't you?"

"Everyone says." I finished my coffee and set the cup on the ground. "In San Francisco I was often mistaken for sunny weather."

"Mark Twain?"

I nodded. We'd read his books together as children.

WHAT I LOVED most when I was young, eight or nine years old, was sitting on the screened-in porch when it rained. I'd take books out there and read for a while, then cover up with a blanket and sit for as long as I could in semi-darkness listening to the rain. The porch had a flat roof. Rain pounded at it like heavy footsteps. And sometimes rain fell in hard waves, advancing then retreating. For the minutes or half-hour it lasted, before one of them found me there, I was shut away from the world, alone, wonderfully alone, and yet somehow intimately a part of it.

OUR MOTHER'S NAME was Lydia. Photographs show her as a tallish, thin woman favoring long skirts and men's blue dress shirts. Her hair was light brown, her eyes green or hazel. The music she liked was Django Reinhardt, big band, Bessie Smith. This I know from her record albums, which I still have, though Dan and I own nothing on which we can play them.

She lingered on a few months after giving birth. For the whole of the time (and this I know from my father, told me as he himself many years later lay dying) she diminished visibly day to day, hour to hour. What color she had left to her skin faded away until, as he said, you could not tell her body from the sheet it lay upon. In the final weeks she lay immobile as a fallen tree, eyes open and directed unblinking to the ceiling. "She had been used up," my father said.

Used up.

Years were to pass, of course, before Lesley and I would come to the realization that in a limited, far more controlled manner, the same thing was being done to ourselves—that we were being used to the identical end.

Later still, I would have cause to wonder at the form my own engagement with the world took. Was I, sitting in seclusion staring out at the world, picking selectively at it, pulling out only those strands I wished, or needed, to get by, boiling them down to a thin gruel of news—was I much different from him?

"THEY'RE CALLED PLEATS. Pleats or ribs. Those ridges running vertically along the cactus. If the pleats constrict, grow closer together, the plant needs water. If they expand, move apart, then it's healthy. Water's everything out here, of course."

"You've fallen in love with it, haven't you? Made this bleak landscape yours."

There are pauses everywhere. One of us speaks and we wait before speaking again. Moments pass between the smallest of events: another hawk banks out over the hill, a rabbit shows itself at house's edge, then for a while nothing happens. Even the sun seems to rest between steps down the sky.

"I suppose I have. There's a beauty to it that most people don't see. A kind of purity and majesty in there being so little, and in life being so difficult."

I gestured to the stand of saguaros on the hill, looking for a moment, with my arm upraised, like one of them.

"Those, for instance. Some of them will grow to forty feet, but the growth is heartbreakingly slow. A ten-year-old saguaro may be only inches tall. In a hundred and fifty years, if against all odds it somehow manages to survive, it finally reaches full height. It's truly majestic then. Nothing like it exists anywhere. Fifty years later it dies.

"Once each spring, in a six-week period just after the desert wildflower season, the saguaros bloom. Just once. Bright red flowers burst from the top of the trunk and tips of the arms. The flowers endure maybe twenty-four hours. They open at night and then, during the day's heat, close."

A light went on in the house. Dan came into view behind the window. He had changed into twill slacks and a pink cotton sweater, loafers without socks. He stood rummaging through our collection of CDs, looked out at me briefly and smiled.

"I still can't believe that you of all people make your living as a journalist."

"Nor can I. One of life's minor absurdities, but an absurdity nonetheless. Still, everything's there on the net somewhere. On the services, in various archives and special-interest cul de sacs. I only have to go in, find what I need. It's all a matter of organization—just like living things getting by out here. Newsmen are forever priding themselves on their objectivity, on being unbiased. 'Even an opinion is a kind of action.' You can't get much more objective or unbiased than someone completely removed from the scene."

"From more than the scene."

I nodded. "I have what I need."

"No. You have what you have to have. The barest minimum."

"It's by choice, Lesley."

After a moment I could see her let it go.

"I'm beat," she said. "If I leave now, I may actually make it to the bed before I drop."

"I'm glad you decided to stay here with us. It's been good."

"It has, hasn't it?"

She started away and turned back. When our eyes met,

for a moment something of the old connection, the palest, trailing ghost of it, leapt into the space between us, then just as quickly was gone. I could see that she had felt it as I did, and felt now, again, the ache and enduring loss of it.

My sister turned again to move towards the house. Day's heat shimmered around her body like an aura, as though she had been trimmed with rough scissors from some other world and laid imperfectly into this one.

THE TURNING POINT, for all of us, came on the night of a spectacularly beautiful day. Lesley and I (I don't recall if for some special occasion) had been taken for a rare outing to a park many miles away, terraces of slender grass sloping gently towards a lake in which ducks swam, from time to time shoveling their bills into the muck at water's edge, then raising them high like jazz trumpeters to toss them from side to side. Allowed to range about for several hours at liberty, in late afternoon we were fed a picnic meal, cold meats and cheeses and fruit, bread and a thermos of sweet tea emerging miraculously from Nurse's wicker basket, before being fetched back home. Nurse, who had come to live with us just after Mother's death looking (as I recall) quite young, by this time had begun looking old.

Perhaps the very beauty of the day, or its singularity, became a deciding point. Perhaps, like myself, Lesley had taken note that day of the changes in Nurse, and this fed her, Lesley's, resolve. It had been, at any rate, building up in her for a long time.

Nurse delivered us to Father, who in turn, saying how much we had been missed, took us into our brother's room. The Frog Prince lay immobile on his bed, pale and waxlike. Surely he was finally dead: I thought this each time. Then as we drew near he began to move, feebly at first, and always without purpose or direction, but ever more strongly at our approach. We felt again the familiar stirring in our mind—pigeon's wings in the attic, Lesley called them.

"No," Lesley said quietly beside me. Then, as Father's face and my own turned to her, she said it again, louder this time: "No!"

She stepped close, staring down at him. The Frog Prince began to beat his stubby doll's arms against himself, rolled his bloated body from side to side the few degrees he was able to manage. His turtlelike head came up, searching blindly.

My sister's eyes grew hard, furious. Even I could feel now the savagery of what she was doing.

She stepped close again, directly over him now.

"You want to live through me? You want to feel what I feel? Then here it is, you monster! Take it! Take it!"

She had thrown open the floodgates of her anger, her hatred, her fury, and it poured out at him, it swept over him, it submerged him.

"You have no right to my life!"

Father, recovering from the shock and realizing what was happening, stepped behind her, roughly seized her and began pulling her away. Intent as she was on inundating the figure on the bed before her, she made no struggle.

"*Do not ever touch me again like that,*" my sister said. The Frog Prince's movements had grown feeble. Then, almost at the moment Father dragged my sister bodily from the room, those movements ceased.

As, I must admit, did my own.

I lay unmoving, barely breathing, I am told, for just over two weeks. Perhaps after all we all three possessed something of that ability by which the Frog Prince pursued what life he had; perhaps Lesley learned to tap into it, used it that one time, against him, and never used it again. Or perhaps she only waited until he was drawing from us those emotions and sensations upon which he thrived, until he was open to her, and then, turning his very hunger against him, overwhelmed him.

Perhaps, like him, and by much the same mechanism, I had absorbed the blows of her fury. Or perhaps (as she insists) I was but exercising for the first time in summary manner my "genius for withdrawal."

Parallax.

How can we ever know just what happened in that room? And if we did, if somehow we came to understand, would anything be, would anything have been, different, changed in any essential way by that understanding?

When I woke, at any rate, when the world began to come back to me, or I to the world, my sister was beside me.

"You're okay," she said.

I nodded.

"I'm leaving," she said.

I knew that, of course.

Our eyes met. The world swam out of focus as we connected—then I fell, flailing, back into it as the connection was gone, severed. It felt as though I were plunging headlong into a pit, and barely managed to catch myself in time. Never in my life before that instant had I known what it was to be truly, finally, unutterably alone. All about me doors closed, ships pulled out to sea, the faces of those I loved looked out the windows of departing trains.

"You'll stay?" she said.

I nodded.

She had known that, of course.

We regarded one another for a moment longer before she turned and walked swiftly away. The door to my room closed like a benediction.

I had inherited the castle.

NIGHT, TOO, WHEN it ended.

After dinner, after dark, we got into the car to return to the hospital. Lesley and I sat in back. Dan drove, as ever, steadily and sure, relaxing into the task, looking about at coal-black mountains in the distance, at the scrub, prickly pear and cholla closer in. He had the radio on, but turned so low I could hardly make out the music. Some sort of soft jazz. There was little enough traffic that car lights, when they broke across us, startled. We rode as through a diorama of civilization's slow gathering: raw, bare earth, an isolated house or two then a string of them, small settlements, finally the outskirts of the city.

Our talk was of tangible things: the meal we'd eaten and the smell of nights out here, our car, the house Lesley had recently bought back in Atlanta.

"There's a room built on top, just this one huge room, like some kind of tower or turret added on, so that it's the whole of the second floor. It has windows in each wall, four of them side by side. I walked into that room for the first time late one afternoon with the sun coming in at a slant, like water thrown across the boards of the floor, and I knew I had to have it. I wound up buying the house for that room."

At length we pulled into the hospital's deserted parking lot. Half a dozen or so vapor lamps set far apart and high on poles gave off a silvery light, sculpting the dark stretch of cement into something lunar. By contrast the corridors of the hospital itself were awash with white, bright as the bridge of a ship. The nurse at her station looked up and shook her head as we drew close, stepping out from behind the high counter to tell us how glad she was that we came when we did. The doctor had just been with him. He would be at rest soon.

Indicating that he would wait out here, Dan settled into a chair by an oval window looking down on the lot we'd just left. Lesley and I went together into the room. His head turned towards us as we entered.

Without speaking, we walked to him, Lesley to the right, myself to the left, and took his hands. His head went from side to side, just as those ducks' heads had done so long ago, from one of us to the other, though of course he couldn't see us. He was weak now, very weak, but as he struggled to summon what strength remained to him, to pull together these last fragments of his talent or his curse or whatever it had been, we both felt it. Felt him reach out to us. Felt things moving deep within us, rearranging there. Felt ourselves connected again, connected forever, as we stood there above his body.

"He's gone," Lesley said.

"Yes."

In the corner, a final bloom burst from the tip of one of the branches, red against the rest's ghostly white.

I looked back at my sister. Tears were in her eyes. I saw them through my own.

Autumn Leaves

THE CALL I never expected would actually come came at 4:32 one Tuesday morning. I hung up and went to the closet for my bag. It had been in there, packed, for well over six years. Karyn sat propped in bed watching, eyes huge. She knew what this meant, and not to ask more. "I'll call when I can," I said. After a moment, the space between us growing ever larger all the while, she nodded. Half an hour later I was in a military helicopter thwacking its way out of the city over rivers and inlets and down the coastline. There were four of us aboard. The pilot had a scrubbed, pink, midwestern look about him. You could have impaled olives on his brush cut.

"So you're one of the doctors."

I wasn't, I was a nurse with some very special training who with the phone's first ring had gone from being one among thousands of faceless health-care workers—in my case, taking care of terminal cancer patients, children mostly—to Authority. But those who trained us down in Virginia taught us that people were happier thinking what they wanted to think and it was to our advantage to let them do so, so I nodded.

Outside Washington we joined a dozen or so others and enplaned for the long haul. Boxed chicken lunches and sacks of little bottles of booze were passed around. Cans of beer in a full-size refrigerator and fresh-brewed coffee in an urn half as large waited our beck and call, we were told. A few had brought books: *Forensics for the General Practitioner*, *Getting Along with Heart Disease*, a Tom Clancy thriller, a novel whose bright white teeth and drops of blood looked as though they might slide off the slick cover into the reader's lap at any moment. The rest of us sat staring into space, minds as full as expressions were empty. I found some back corner of my brain providing words for the music playing quietly over the sound system.

Since you went away, the days grow long. . . .

Our training was as specific as it was thorough. Four, five doctors in the whole country might be able to identify, say, bubonic plague if they saw it. But every last one of us would immediately recognize signs and symptoms of anthrax, smallpox, typhoid, Ebola and half a dozen others. Incubation times, vectors, previous outbreaks or occurences, possible vaccines and treatments were engraved in the very folds of our brains. We came on the scene, it got handed over to us, baby, bath water and all. Local police and officials, medical personnel, military—everyone deferred.

I'd been in New Orleans a couple of times before, once back around century's end with Karyn for the Jazz Festival, once during training. The country's sole remaining leprosarium was in Louisiana, and instructors brought us down to see things firsthand. The city had always looked ancient, blasted, and at first there seemed little difference: abandoned, half-gutted buildings, heaps of trash, mattresses and dead animals at curbside. Then you realized almost no one was on the streets.

Military trucks carted us in from the city's outskirts along water's edge to Camp Alpha. Off to each side all the way, close by and in the middle distance, black smoke rose from fires. The few civilian vehicles we encountered pulled off the road to let us pass. The city had become a patchwork of camps, this the largest of them, acre upon acre of tents, lean-tos and sheds running over the low wall right up to Lake Ponchartrain and back onto what had long been the city's dearest real estate. Officials had set up HQ in a house designed by Frank Lloyd Wright. It was bone white, a thing of curves, and looked like a huge ship, complete with foredeck, gone aground among trees. Autodidact James K. Feibleman, a millionaire without formal training or degree who'd become head of Tulane's philosophy department, had lived here, as had writer wife Shirley Ann Grau and writer son Peter. Tulane's campus, meanwhile, along with that of Loyola and adjoining Audubon Park with its hundred-year-old water oaks, had become another sprawling tent city.

Briefing took place in what was once the kitchen of Feibleman's home. Dozens of folding chairs had butts holding them down. The rest of us spilled out, sitting, standing, propped against walls, through sliding doors onto the patio as Dr. Fachid Ramadan, all four-feet-six of him, bustled to the room's front, by the monolith of the refrigerator's stainless-steel door.

"We do not know what it is," he said without preamble, eyes large as globes behind thick eyeglasses, "though of course we are hoping all of you will be able to help us with this." His phrases had an intrinsic rhythm to them, a quiet rise and fall, as though he were reading poetry. "This could scarcely be more confusing, more difficult to get a handle on. Yes—as I know many of you are about to ask—at this point we *are* assuming a seeding. Undifferentiated flulike symptoms at first. Slow gather, sudden crash. By the time you admit that you and loved ones are sick, it is too late." He went on to detail our small fund of actual information, providing a long, intricate list of possible signs and symptoms, a checklist of similarities and divergence from disease processes with which we were all familiar. Poorly spelled and unchecked in the rush, copies of the lists floated onto a projector screen behind him as he spoke.

I held up my hand:

"Vectors?"

"We do not know. Not airborne—we are fairly certain of this. Direct contact, bodily fluids. Insects have yet to be ruled out. A handful of cases may be traceable to rodents. Squirrels, nutria."

"Staff?" I asked.

"None yet. But we barely have our feet in the door. I was on site in Malaysia, was fetched by Air Force officials and flown here. This was forty-six hours ago. I have been a stranger to pillows since. We have no idea what the incubation period might be."

First rule: Expect the worst.

And we did—though ultimately expectation and imagination proved as unequal to the challenge as did our knowledge.

Having gone through the program together and been for the duration propinquitous friends, despite a dozen or so dinners and wine-soft evenings in the mix, Sara Freedman and I had little reason ever to anticipate seeing one another again. Now we walked along the river's slow curve carrying kebobs bought from street vendors where Café du Monde used to be and a bottle of Chilean Merlot. Carrying lots of things. And talking with a freedom and absolute lack of self-consciousness I thought left behind forever, shed skin of adolescence, telling one another secrets, fears.

"Not a good idea under the circumstances," I remarked when Sara dangled feet, sandals and all, in the water. But when she pointed out that every day we were smack among the actual as opposed to the theoretical, I relented, feeling foolish.

"This river used to be filled with boats," I said. "Coming in from the Gulf, heading up to Natchez and Memphis and St. Louis. For three hundred years."

No boats now. Only trash, dead fish, bloated human bodies. They floated, careened spinning from bank to bank, lazily, as though in a dream.

"Things change."

"I don't think the word *change* covers what's happening now."

"Maybe nothing does."

It was fall—have I mentioned that? Leaves gone crimson and gold on the trees even this far south. I hungered for New England autumns, feet shuffling through layers of ankle-deep leaves. Our bodies have those same changes as voids within them, waiting.

"I've thought of you, you know," Sara said. "Often, and fondly."

I passed her a kebob. A chunk of cucumber. Levered out the cork and poured wine into plastic cups. We sat without speaking. At water's edge, a line of ants methodically dismembered a sphinx moth's body and carried it off. Two others, one pushing, one pulling, steadily moved along a chunk of celery easily twenty times their size. Stew for dinner?

Maybe it was their time now.

We'd lost a dozen or more the night before. Toward dawn I was awakened by one of the nurses, knowing as I opened my eyes that it wasn't yet daylight, knowing little else. I'd been asleep just under two hours, she told me, and she was sorry, but the boy was having trouble breathing. The boy was nineteen. We'd watched other members of his department go down one by one, till he was the only one remaining, de facto sheriff. Terror in his eyes. Just past dawn, the terror passed as he joined the others.

Later that night, both sleepless, Sara and I wandered at the same time into the kitchen. Without speaking she turned and leaned across the counter. I pulled down her shorts just far enough, ground into her soundlessly from behind as she watched our single shadow on the wall, but could not stay hard. Around us everywhere the cries and moans of those in our care.

Two months later I'd fly out by copter, hauled above and across the dead city by the machine's brute force, New Orleans now like nothing so much as the still, crumbling husk of an insect. I'd remember how, as I came here on the plane, *Autumn Leaves* was playing: *Since you went away . . .* In memory, in the weeks I had left, Sara's face would look up at me again and again as she struggled for breath, and again and again I'd place a hand on hers. I never called Karyn. She was gone by the time I got back. Gone like Sara.

That morning in the copter I would remember an old song by Woodie Guthrie, something I'd not thought of in twenty years. Field workers had been brought in from Mexico and, their job done, put on a plane to be sent back. But the plane caught fire over Los Gatos Canyon.

Who are these friends who are falling like dry leaves?
The radio says they're just deportees.

We're all itinerants, shipped in, trucked away once the work's done. Dry leaves. Autumn leaves. Everything leaves. Everything leaves, everything changes. Treasure the margins while they last, treasure everything that sinks into the blur, treasure it all.

Treasure it all.

The Monster in Mid-Life

"I FIND IT harder and harder to get my work done," the creature said.

We had arranged to meet in a small but charming café near the river, one of several where I'm known to staff, and where a café crème appeared magically before me as I took my seat. Three women sat at the table nearest us, one of them gaunt, ascetic and unsmiling as though set upon refusing all life's pleasures, the others full-figured, laughing, eating. Half a meter further along, a hideous small dog on a pink leash peed against the ornamental railing that divided café from sidewalk.

"It's what you were created for," I said.

"But without commitment—without soul, if you will—what joy can there be in it? Only gestures, hollow forms. . . ."

The creature's hand, reaching for the cup of latte, capsized it. Those claws, so useful for rending and tearing, were poorly adapted to such mundane use. They clattered against the table top as the creature gathered up a handful of napkins to mop the spill.

"Sure you won't have a bite to eat?" I said.

"I would not turn away another cup of coffee. And I would promise to take better care of this one."

"*Encore*," I told Marcel as he passed by. Briefly he glanced towards the creature, who attempted a smile. When it did, its eyes became vertical slits; a low moan, perhaps a growl, issued involuntarily from its throat.

"For a long time, you understand," the creature said, "that was enough. I went on doing what I was best at, what I was meant for. Then, slowly, I began to sense there might be something more."

"We all have these moments. There are no straight lines in nature. Nor, for the most part, in our lives."

"You are correct in this, I am certain."

The creature's eyes fixed on the dog who, having finished emptying its bladder against the railing, now began yipping at a nearby pigeon. Pigeon and dog were roughly of a size. The dog's owner, a woman of forty or more in a flower-print dress, was off by the bus stop, leaning into a departing lover like a book from whose shelf other, adjacent books have been removed.

"Unlike you, I was not created to live with doubt."

Absentmindedly the creature reached down to scoop up the dog and popped the wriggling, whimpering thing into its mouth, tossing the leash, this tiny pink lariat, back out onto the sidewalk.

"As I said, I find it increasingly difficult to get my work done, harder each day to find within myself the proper drive and motivation. Besides—" His eyes swept café, street, city beyond. "— there is so much evil in the world now. Am I truly of use any longer? Perhaps I am . . . unnecessary now. Perhaps the purpose for which I was created *is* no more."

He emitted what may have been a sigh, or the resounding of some intestinal transaction.

"You understand, I have known all along that it would never be for me to have a settled life, to come home from work at day's end and find shelter there, to dream. For me there has been only this."

Holding out his hand, he closed it into a fist. Claws curled above the fist like the petals of some exotic plant.

"I don't have answers for you," I said. "One goes on with it all, goes through the motions, carries on. With luck, eventually, it all adds up to something."

Around us, subtly, darkness grew, daylight tucking itself in at the corners of buildings. The woman in the flower-print dress stood holding the empty pink leash, looking vacantly at it, as into the frame of a broken mirror. Café Mir sits at one of the city's major crossroads. Southward now, filtering in from uptown, filed a line of protestors carrying anti-abortion signs; around their necks hung those bright red personal bombs sold almost everywhere nowadays. Up another street, emerging from Old City, marched a group of young women dressed all in black. Glittery X's were painted across their breasts. Trousers bore cartoonlike, stylized penises done in the same medium.

"It appears I am needed," the creature said. "Thank you for coming."

I waved my hand to indicate that it was nothing.

The creature stood. "Whatever else we may say of it, the world does keep offering up delicious choices," it said.

I nodded and started off in the opposite direction. I had work to see to, also, of course. My own delicious choices to make.

The Museum of Last Week

THORNTON IS RIGHT. The park has become crowded, all but impassable, inhabited by thickets of statues in various stages of self-creation and decay. I had no idea there were so many of them. Unmoving bodies as far as can be seen, crowded up against one another, standing, stooping, stretching. Some on their backs. The children like to come in at night and topple them.

I walked by there today. Not that I'd meant or planned to. Far from it. Nonetheless, stomach rumbling and sour with the morning's coffee, I found myself outside the fence looking in.

Scant miles away, scattered about with cholla and bottlebrush cactus, the desert looms, a sea bottom forsaken by the sea.

It is, yes, beginning to look like her, just as Thornton said. In a few days the features will be unmistakeable. Even as I watched—though in truth I must admit I stood there for some time—they changed.

Tell me you won't forget me, you said.

Easy enough, Julie. How could I ever? Ravage of your face in those last months soon to be caught in that of the statue inside, by the concrete bench and the fountain that hasn't worked for years.

The whole secret of everything, you once told me—art, conversation, life itself—is where the accent's placed: the emphasis, the stress.

Do things happen faster now, closer together, than they used to, or does it just seem that way? As though all has shifted to time-lapse photography, entire life cycles come and gone in moments; as though the lacunae and longueurs that for the most part comprise our lives, these struts that hold up the scaffold of the world, have been removed. Our lives have become instant nostalgia, an infinite longing for what's been lost. While the world, like Wallace Stevens' wide-mouthed jar left out in the rain, slowly fills to the brim with the momentos, decay and detritus of our past.

Looking for more coffee, hair of the dog, I stop at a convenience store. I always order two cups, and sure enough, as I depart, a youngish man in corduroy sportcoat and chinos approaches, coat so worn as to resemble a chenille bedspread, chinos eaten away well above onetime cuffs.

"I am attempting to resolve the categorical imperative with the categorically impossible," he tells me. We stand staring at one another. Kant at ten in the morning on the streets of downtown Phoenix. "Do you have the time, sir?" he says after a moment.

Professing that I wear no watch, I offer what I have instead: the extra coffee.

"I only wish I could have the luxury of not knowing," he says. "Unfortunately that is not the case. And I feel," he says as he takes a sip of coffee and falls in beside me, "that there may not be much time left." We stride along, two men of purpose moving through city, day and world. Perhaps every third sentence of what he says makes sense. He is desperate for bus fare to the university where he teaches, one of these vagarious sentences informs me. "I was lost but now am found. Still, yesterday and today, I have had no access to research facilities." And a bit later on: "Tomorrow for the first time my students will be prepared for class and I will not be."

I ask what he teaches.

"History. And, every other semester, a seminar on forgetfulness."

Not long towards nightfall, I attend a housewarming for Sara and Seth, researchers who have just moved in together. This is a match made somewhere just off the interstate between Heaven and Hollywood. Seth is the world's leading authority on mucus, can speak for hours concerning protein content, viscosity, adhesiveness, mucopurulence, degrees of green. Sara in turn has fifty pounds of elephant penis in her—now their—refrigerator.

You once told me that we understand the world, we organize it, in whatever manner we're able.

"An erect elephant penis weighs around 108 pounds and is 62 inches in length," says Gordon, who, as an editor, knows such things.

"That's up to here," Ralph remarks, holding his hand at a level about six inches above my head. Flamingly gay, he takes inordinate delight in such rodomontade.

"Sixty-two inches is five-foot-two, " I remark.

"Right," Ralph says. "Up to here on you," indicating again the same spot.

What does it mean, I wonder, that he feels this need to belittle me during an exchange concerning penises? But I suppose that indeed I will be, must be, a short statue. Julie will tower over me as she did in life, in every way.

Correct me if I'm wrong, but this is how I remember it. Gregory Peck, on safari, has been injured. He lies all but helpless in his tent, gangrene staking claim to leg and life as hyenas circle outside. The woman he loves attends him.

This is what I'm thinking as I step away from others, away from fifty pounds of elephant penis in the fridge and dissertations on mucus, into the night. I was eight, nine, when I first saw that movie at the Paramount one Sunday afternoon. Scant blocks away the Mississippi boiled in its banks. Within the week it would surmount levee and sandbags and rush the lowlands. I kept having to ask my brother to explain what was going on in the movie. I'm not sure he understood a great deal more than I did at that point, but he gave it his best. He's now a philosopher.

And now, of course, in our world, anticipation has gone into overdrive. Gregory Peck would never just lie there listening to the hyenas. They'd be on him before he knew it.

Back home, I brew white tea (high in antioxidants, low in caffeine) in a white pot and take it in a white cup out onto my white-pine patio. Darkness surrounds, and I lift my cup to it—whether in supplication or challenge I do not know. What has my life come to? What have all our lives, what has our world, come to?

I go back inside, to the pantry. I've saved these a long time.

The scars come in packages of six. I rip open a package at random and sense the scars's restlessness as they stir to life, sense their pleasure at being allowed to do at last what they were created for.

The Genre Kid

SAMMY LEVISON WAS fourteen when he discovered that he could shit little Jesuses. They were approximately three inches tall and perfectly formed, right down to the beard and a suggestion of folds in the robe. Tiny eyes looked out appealingly; one hand was lifted in peaceful greeting. The first came incidentally, but all that was required to repeat the performance, he found, was concentration. Later on, Sammy tried pushing out little Buddhas and Mohammeds, but it wasn't the same. He didn't understand that.

His mother had been brushing her hair at the sink and, walking past as he stood, caught sight of what was in the bowl. Her hand shot out to restrain his own from flushing. A miracle, she said, it's a miracle—and called his father. She didn't go to work at the laundry that day. When he got home from school, the line of neighbors and supplicants ran for a block or more along the street, up stairs, and down the hallway to his open door. One by one, as at televised funeral processions, the line advanced as people filed through the two cramped rooms shared by mother, father, brother, sister and Sammy, to the toilet, to have a look. Many crossed themselves. Not a few appealed to the bobbing figure for relief, cessation of pain, succor. Every so often the little Jesus would move in the bowl and there would be sharp intakings of breath.

Soon Sammy had become a frequent guest on local talk shows, within the year a guest on national versions of the same, holding forth on all manner of subjects, northern Ireland, capital punishment, the Israeli stalemate, of which he knew nothing at all. Professors, priests and politicos, vapid interviewers whose perfect teeth were set like jewelry into bright, enthusiastic smiles, simple men of God with lacquered hair—all mused on what Sammy might be considered to be: a messenger, an artist, a devil, a saint. Though everyone knew, the precise occasion for his being here or being under discussion, what he actually *did*, got mentioned only obliquely.

Anchormen and –women never blinked, of course, this being only a storm-tossed version of what had been drilled into them at journalism school: to make tidy small packages, to sketch and color in the rude outline of actuality without ever once enclosing the beast itself. Their faces registered concern as they listened to Sammy's supposed confessions. On camera they crossed legs and leaned close, fiddled Mont Blanc pens between fingers like batons, wands, instruments of thought.

Mother didn't have to go back to work at the laundry. Father bought up block after block of apartment buildings, a scattering of convenience stores previously owned by immigrants, waste-disposal companies. Brothers and sisters attended the best, most expensive schools. And one day in his own fine home, there among tongue and groove hardwood floors, imported Spanish tile, exquisite bathroom fixtures, Sammy found himself costive—unable to perform, as it were.

He was the best at what he did. Actually, since he was the world's first coprolitist, he was the *only* one who did what he did. But Sammy wanted something *more*.

Meanwhile he was blocked.

"I have to follow where my talent takes me," he said, "I have to be true to it," as he sat, grunting, "I can't just go on endlessly doing what I already know how to do, what I've done before."

With his absence from the scene Sammy had become something of a ripe mystery, raw ingredient for the cocktail shakers of media myth. WHERE IS SAMMY L? a ten-minute segment of one prime-time show asked, clock ticking ominously in the background. Newsmen with perfect teeth leaned over words such as *angst, noblesse oblige* and *hubris*, bringing them back to life with mouth-to-mouth and sending viewers off in search of long-forgotten dictionaries. T-shirts with Sammy's picture fore and aft began appearing everywhere.

The first of his new issue were malformed, misbegotten things.

"We claim there's freedom, tell ourselves this is the country that gave freedom to the world," Sammy said in a rare interview from this period. "There's no freedom here. As artists we have two choices. Either we plod down roads preordained by those in power, the rich, the yea-sayers, arbiters of taste, style and custom; or we cater to the demands of the great unwashed, trailer-park folk, the lumpen proletariat," sending viewers and research assistants alike again in search of those dictionaries.

Gradually over time Sammy's new creations began to take on a form of their own. At first, like the boulders of Stonehenge and menhirs of Carnac, these forms were rough-hewn, lumpen themselves in fact, more presence than image; and even once realized, were like forms no one had seen before, troubling, disturbing.

By this time, of course, the headlights of media attention had swung elsewhere, found new deer. There was, a few years further along, with *Famous Men*, his exhibit of images of Holocaust victims, a brief return to representation and an even briefer rekindling of media interest; then silence. All the things for which an artist labors, depth, control, subtlety, he had attained, but no one would see these.

"Perhaps this is as it should be," Sam Levison said. "We practice our art, if we are serious artists, finally for ourselves alone, *within* ourselves alone."

And so he did, to the point that the Times' obituary identified him simply as "Samuel Levison, 48, of Crook Bend near Boston, eccentric, hermit and performance artist whose work endured its fifteen minutes of fame and passed from view as though with a great sigh of relief."

At least they'd used the word *great*.

In the garage apartment where he spent his last years, nothing was found of whatever new work may have taken up the artist's life in the decades since the fall. Half-hearted rumors sprang up that he'd destroyed it all, or had pledged his sister to do so. Appropriately enough, Sam offered no last words, only one final creation pushed out as he died. This was, as in the early days, a small Jesus. Sam's landlord, come yet again to try and collect rent, found it there as, later, he waited for the ambulance, and picked it up. But its eyes bored into him and would not let go. After a moment he dropped it back to the floor and crushed it with his foot.

Telling Lives

A COUPLE OF kids are standing at the bus stop reading my book about Henry Wayne, possibly a school assignment. Henry's right there with them with a cup of coffee from the Circle K, answering questions. So probably it's an assignment, all right. The city bus pulls in and they get on. I'm never sure how this works. Do they get some kind of pass to ride the city bus to school or what? Every morning there's a couple dozen of them out there waiting.

Across the street, Stan Baker, who owns most of the good affordable apartments in this part of town, is up on the roof of one of his units poking around at ledges, fittings, tar. Someone else with khakis and a clipboard is up there with him. City employee's my guess. Stan waves when I look up. I wrote my first biography about him.

No one ever imagined they'd catch on this way. Who could have? I wrote that first one, about Stan, on a lark, more or less to have something to do as I sat in front of the computer each morning. My last, literary novel, at which I'd labored a full year, had sunk without a trace, not even flotsam or driftwood left behind. I'd taught for a while at the local community college but had no real taste or aptitude for it. When I went on to write features for the *Daily Republic*, bored with simple transcription, I found myself first making up details, then entire stories. It was in the biographies, cleaving to the well-defined shoreline of a life, that I found a strange freedom, a release.

"Barely scratch beneath the surface of any one of us, even the dullest slob around," my old man used to tell me, "and you'll come onto a source of endless fascination and contradiction. We're all inexhaustible, teeming planets, filled with wonder."

This from a man who had little interest in others' lives (mine included, sadly) and who rarely left the house. Number twenty-two in the series.

Nowadays, of course, the biographies are about all anyone around here reads. Has the town somehow found itself, come to itself, within them? Certainly, for my part, I've stumbled onto an inexhaustible supply of material—and my life's work.

Carefree, the town where they care.

That's how we're known now, here just down the road from the nation's sixth largest city with its riot of dun-colored buildings, cloverleafs and sequestered communities, ridgeback of mountains looming always in the distance.

And we do care. All of us, every one. School kids with their backpacks and mysterious piercings, bank presidents, sanitation-truck jockeys, yardmen and insurance salesmen alike. Clerks at convenience stores going nine out of ten falls with the angel of English each moment of their day. The group of street dwellers who regularly congregate in the alley behind Carta de Oro.

However we try to break out, to break free, we're forever locked within our own minds. Locked away from knowledge of ourselves every bit as much. But there's this one ride out we can sometimes hitch, this tiny window through which with luck and good weather we can peer and see ourselves, in the guise of another, looking back in.

That's what the biographies have become for us, I think, those rides, those windows.

"Hard at work, I see," Bobby Taylor (number eighteen in the series) says as I sip my morning double espresso at The Coffee Grinder. He's on duty, has his helmet tucked under one arm, what looks like half a gallon of coffee in the other hand, motorcycle pulled up just outside.

"Finger on the pulse and all that, Officer."

"Looks more like butt in chair to me."

"What can I say? It's a sedentary occupation."

"How's your mom?"

Mother had been hospitalized six months back after meeting a UPS man at the door with an electric carving knife. She said he'd raped her, and no one should treat a twelve-year-old that way. In hospital, or so she claimed, she'd turned thirteen. One of the nurses baked her a cake, and everyone gathered round for the party. She'd blown out all thirteen candles.

"Holding her own."

"Alzheimer's, right?"

"What they say."

"She know you?"

"Some days she does."

"Next time you visit and it's one of those days, tell her little Bobby Taylor says hello. Had her for tenth-grade English, like nearly everyone else in town. Only 'A' I ever got. Parents couldn't decide whether to be shocked or expect it go on happening."

"And?"

"Shocked won out."

I was getting ready to leave when a thirtyish woman stepped up to my table. She had black hair cut short in the back, longer towards the front, giving an impression of two wings.

"Mr. Warren?"

"Yes."

She held out a warm, narrow hand, nails painted white and trimmed square across.

"Justine Driscoll. May I join you?"

Although I'd not noticed it before this, a radio was playing behind the counter. Now soft jazz gave way to news. I heard "two fairies collided off the coast of Maine," then realized the announcer meant *ferries*.

"Please do. Can I get you something?"

"I'm fine. I own a small publishing company, Mr. Warren. I was wondering if—"

"I have an exclusive contract with McKay and Rosenwald, you must know that."

"Of course. But I hoped you might look this over. It's our leader for the fall. A flagship book, really, launching a new series."

From a bookbag slung like a purse over one shoulder she extracted and passed across a copyedited manuscript, corrections and emendations in red pencil in a tiny, tidy hand.

I read the first few pages.

"The barber's hair," I said.

It began with the story of my mother at the hospital, blowing out those thirteen candles.

"You're not surprised."

"It was only a matter of time."

"Would you be willing to give it a read, let us know if there are errors?"

I pushed it back across the table. "I have no wish to read it, Miss Driscoll. You have my blessing, though—for whatever that's worth."

"Actually, it's worth quite a lot. Thank you."

She stashed the manuscript back in her book bag.

"Our sales people are strong behind this. We have solid orders from Barnes & Noble, Borders."

"Then let me join them to say that I sincerely hope it does well for you."

"I'll not take up any more of your time, Mr. Warren."

She stood. Her eyes swept the room. I had the sense of a camera recording this scene. It was a glance I knew all too well.

"Miss Driscoll?"

She turned back.

"You look remarkably like my wife, Julie. Way you're dressed. Nails. Hair."

"Do I really?"

"She died eight years ago, a suicide."

"I know. From the book. And I'm sorry."

"This Francis Frank, the author. It's you, isn't it?"

She stood, irresolute. Before she could respond I asked, "Do you have plans for the rest of the day?"

"No."

"Yes."

Your New Career

EACH DAY WE'RE required to assume the identity of one of the other students. At first, when we knew so little of one another, it was less difficult, but we're well along in the program now and have gained considerable personal knowledge. On the other hand, all those early, generic assignments, impersonating postmen, policemen and the like, have paid off. This has been going on from the first day. We're graded on how well we bring it off:

Preparation. Equal parts Research (on the internet) and Observation (finding those physical, character and speech traits of the target that others in the class will recognize).

Persuasiveness. This one, like much else in life, is mostly attitude. You must charge right in and right along, pursuing your objective and game plan, oblivious of all objections, challenges, detours and roadblocks.

Perseverance. You do not, whatever happens, surrender. Even in the face of certain defeat, cover hopelessly blown, revealed for what you are, you do not give up the pretense.

Yesterday I received the only 10/10/10 of the semester. Called upon first thing in the morning, I stood, walked to the front of the class and began my presentation, continuing same, with scheduled breaks, of course, until almost five in the afternoon. This time I had become not a fellow student but our instructor, Mr. Soong. As Mr. Soong sat in the back of the classroom smoking cigarette after cigarette and looking ever more nervous, I taught the class he might have taught, sketching out details of a standard shadow-agent operation, citing examples from my own (his own) field work and my (his) personal history.

The secret-agent school is located on a strip mall in the far-southeastern reach of the city, just at the boundary where the city goes down for the third time into suburbs. One end of the mall's held down by a Petsright, the other by an upstart home-supply center. An income-tax service, a cut-rate office-supply store and two food shops, Ted's Fish N Chips, Real-y-Burgers, straggle down the line. Standing apart across a narrow empty lot chockful of go-cups and partial frames of shopping carts like disabled vehicles left behind on battlefields, a shabby cinema plays last year's forgotten films at a dollar a shot to sparse audiences of forgotten people.

"A moment, if you will," Mr. Soong announced as, taking my seat near day's end, I passed both torches, classroom and identity, back to him. He held up a finger profoundly nicotine-stained to the first joint and only seriously stained to the next—a characteristic of which I had made full use. By now, mindful of rush hour, students are compulsively checking watches as though they're detonation devices. The next wave of hopefuls, buying their way towards certification as nursing assistants, teems on the sidewalk outside. The storefront classroom's on time-share between various vocational schools. Stuck in a dead-end job?, You're only ninety days away from an exciting career as _____, You can make the difference, etc.

"Violence, I'm afraid, has paid a visit," Mr. Soong said, British locution and Indian rhythm chiming together like two dice in a cup. "At or about one o'clock this morning, noticing that lights remained on well after hours, a squad car on routine patrol pulled up in front of the Rialto." Everyone hereabouts called it The Real Toe. "One officer stayed behind to radio in, the other went into the lobby. There he found a young man—the assistant manager as it turned out, an eighteen-year-old who closed each night after seeing the rest of the staff out—lying in front of the popcorn machine, quite dead."

Lying in a pool formed of blood and piss in equal parts, with a small pool of Real Butter Flavoring nearby, lesser lake among the greater—but Mr. Soong doesn't say this.

"Both the mall's proprietors and school officials have asked that I urge you all to exercise caution today as you leave. Please do so." That index finger went up again, pointing to the sky like a saint's. "Observe the buddy system." Now a second finger. "Be aware always of your surroundings." And a third. "Walk purposefully." Little finger. "Make eye contact with anyone you encounter." Lady Thumb. "Have your car keys out and ready."

Because it was the first Friday of the month, tuition was due. One by one we filed past Mr. Soong's makeshift desk to pay up, settle, render unto Caesar, etc., before filtering out onto the parking lot where a magnificent sunset burgeoned parachutelike above the horizon as the next generation of students prepared to clamber in. Many, as always, paid in cash. Some, surely, are illegal; others, for whatever and various reasons, have or lay claim to no bank accounts.

I sat in my car smoking a last cigarette, radio tuned to the local NPR, as late arrivals rushed from car to classroom in search of the excellent salary and fulfilling career promised them by late-night TV ads, and as day's parachute collapsed into darkness. At Standard Uniform in Twin Cedars Mall a mile or so further along towards the city, they've all purchased green uniform tops, white shoes, shiny scissors, gleaming stethoscopes. I watched Mr. Soong cross cracked pavement to his yellow Honda. Often, I know, once all are gone, Mr. Soong returns to the classroom to work.

On the way home I listen to an interview with a writer who's published a book about caged birds taken as safeties into coal mines. "Mute, unsocialized birds are best for the purpose," he said. "Mockingbirds with their vast repertoire proved worthless: they sing and sing up till the very moment they keel over."

The color of the universe, another interviewee, a physicist, insists at length, is beige. He also has written a book which expounds his beliefs. The world is fast filling up with news and interviews, books and belief. Soon there'll be no room for people.

Next morning, Miss Smith pulls into the spot alongside as I'm sitting there with windows rolled down listening to bad country music and finishing up my large coffee and egg-and-bacon sandwich. I stopped off at the Greek's diner as always. We go in and find Mr. Soong lying in a pool of sticky red stuff. Soon other students begin arriving; more than one stumbles back outside to throw up.

"Maybe this is our final exam," I say to Miss Smith.

Mr. Soong, get up. Light a cigarette, smile your lopsided smile, and grade me. Tell me how I did.

A City Equal To My Desire

ACKNOWLEDGEMENTS

"Ukulele and the World's Pain" first appeared in Alfred Hitchcock's Mystery Magazine, © 2002.

"Drive" first appeared in Measures of Poison, ed. Dennis McMillan, © 2002.

"When Fire Knew My Name" first appeared on the website Fantastic Metropolis, was reprinted in Redsine, © 2002.

"Get Along Home" first appeared on the website 3 AM Magazine, © 2002.

"Blue Yonders" first appeared on the website Fantastic Metropolis and was reprinted in Ache Magazine, © 2002.

"Stepping Away from the Stone" first appeared in Transversions, © 1999.

"Second Thoughts" first appeared in Lady Churchill's Rosebud Wristlet, © 2000.

"Concerto for Violence and Orchestra" first appeared in Men from Boys, ed. John Harvey, © 2003.

"New Life" first appeared in The Third Alternative, © 2003.

"Roofs and Forgiveness in the Early Dawn" first appeared in Talebones, © 2002.

"Under Construction" first appeared in Crossroads: Southern Stories of the Fantastic, ed. Andy Duncan & F. Brett Cox, © 2004.

"Flesh of Stone and Steel" first appeared in Thirteen: Photographs by Marc Atkins, © 2002.

"Up" first appeared in Leviathan 3, ed. Forrest Aguirre and Jeff VanderMeer, © 2002.

"Day's Heat" first appeared in Asimov's Science Fiction Magazine, © 2001.

"Autumn Leaves" first appeared on the website Fantastic Metropolis and in The Barcelona Review, © 2002.

"The Monster in Mid-Life" first appeared in The Dirty Goat, © 2003.

"The Genre Kid" first appeared in The Magazine of Fantasy & Science Fiction, © 2003.

"Your New Career" first appeared in Crimewave, © 2003.

"The Museum of Last Week" and "Telling Lives" first appeared in Lady Churchill's Rosebud Wristlet, © 2004.

"Christian," "Venice Is Sinking into the Sea" and "Pitt's World" appear here for the first time, © 2004.

The author would also like to thank Anselm Hollo, from one of whose poems the title of this collection derives.

Printed in the United States
22844LVS00001B/148-153